D1130452

WITHDRAWN FROM KENT STATE
UNIVERSITY LIBRARIES

Books by Adrienne Jones

RIDE THE FAR WIND

WILD VOYAGEUR

Wild
Voyageur

Wild
Voyageur

Story of a Canada Goose

by Adrienne Jones

Illustrated by Lois Darling

Little, Brown and Company   *Boston   Toronto*

COPYRIGHT © 1966 BY ADRIENNE JONES

ALL RIGHTS RESERVED. NO PART OF THIS BOOK MAY BE REPRO-
DUCED IN ANY FORM WITHOUT PERMISSION IN WRITING FROM THE
PUBLISHER, EXCEPT BY A REVIEWER WHO MAY QUOTE BRIEF PAS-
SAGES IN A REVIEW TO BE PRINTED IN A MAGAZINE OR NEWSPAPER.

LIBRARY OF CONGRESS CATALOG CARD NO. 66-11005

FIRST EDITION

Published simultaneously in Canada
by Little, Brown & Company (Canada) Limited

PRINTED IN THE UNITED STATES OF AMERICA

To Bobo

KENT STATE UNIVERSITY
LIBRARY
KENT, OHIO
530851

Contents

Wild
Voyageur

1 The Beginning

On a certain day late in May the high-flying V's of Canada geese came in across the cold blue of the arctic sky, black scratches of gabbling sound far above the Mackenzie River delta country.

One big gander heading a large formation of geese slanted his wide, powerful wings in a gliding spiral. The flock turned behind him. His mate flew close by.

These two had been together on ten of the long aerial voyages from Tule Lake in northern California to the shores of the Beaufort Sea on Canada's arctic coast. Ten years, ten flights.

. The gander's bright eyes scanned the land below. This year was a good one. The flood waters from the spring breakup rushed through the many-fingered channel of the Mackenzie delta, pushing the winter ice of the northern sea back from the body of the land, leaving a wide strip of black water along the shore. To help this conquest of the ice, the winds from the south blew their warm breath along the edge of the white sheet that glistened in the May sun, beating the forces of winter back beyond the seventy-fifth parallel. Yes, this was a good spring.

There had been others, cruel ones, when the world stayed white, locked in the embrace of snow and ice, well into June; other springs when the wind from across the polar cap had lashed the land. In those years the big gander and his mate had only the withered grass of the last summer to sustain them until the sun could climb higher up the steep sky, only the withered grass dug with painful effort from beneath the snow to feed their bodies lean and hungry from the long flight.

A good spring, this one. Yet this was to be the gander's last. He was not old, as geese go, perhaps twelve or thirteen seasons, and twenty would not be unusual with luck. Still, this would be his last. For the present though, death was only a shadow across the brightness of the May landscape that now wheeled below them as though it and not they turned and drew near.

As he glided lower, lower, the gander turned his dark head on the long flexible neck to glimpse his mate who flew beside him. The white patch that swept beneath his chin and up each cheek glinted in the light and marked him as a honker, a Canada goose, the largest of the wild geese. The clean gray-brown of his mate's back feathers, the soft gray of her underparts, the strong reaching primaries of her wing tips were clear against the sky. So was the sleek black of her head and neck with the white patch that matched his own, for they were feathered the same, the gander and his goose. As a pair they flew, breaking away from the flock. In the rush of the air they slid downward together.

The land was close beneath them now. There was a thin marbling of brown where the earth was already beginning to show through the snow. It was a good spring. It was also good that the long journey was over for the urge of mating was upon him.

The season for mating, nesting, incubation is short in the north, and for this each year they had risked the early flight into the home of winter, risked the cruel cold and starvation so the new brood would be ready for the flight south before the long arctic night once more held the land.

The wide horizon of the high sky was gone, shrinking in upon them as they glided down; the fingers of the delta grew broad below their vision; the textures of the snow, the rocks, the water were clear, clearer. In moments with a swift swoop and flapping of wings the journey was ended and the tired pinions folded to rest.

The mating was over. On one of the low marshy islands of the delta the gander and his goose had built their nest. This island was toward the perimeter of the delta, and here where the river current was weak the ice of winter still bridged the gap between island and continental shore. From here the shore began its curve away to the west, stretching from the delta out and along the edge of the Beaufort Sea. The land was rich in materials for the building of the nest, and the pair flew together to bring back the sticks, the rushes, the reeds, the grasses and bits of plants. Along the edge of Mackenzie Bay they flew for the sticks of whitened driftwood that had been washed down by the spring floods. They paid no heed to the jaegers, to the kittiwakes, nor to the mother seals and their pups who lay basking on the sea ice in the cool arctic sun. The sticks were gathered and the frame of the nest was made.

From the low growth of the heath, the small brushy shallow-rooted growth that flourished in the scant layer of earth covering the permafrost, the two geese gathered smaller branches and twigs. These were thrust into the driftwood framework, layering the top in a solid mass. In searching for the twiggy sticks of the heath they gave no thought to the ptarmigan, nor the snow bunting, nor the silent arctic fox scraggly now in the process of losing his fine winter coat.

Next came the pliable reeds and rushes from the swampy river delta. These padded and softened the rough frame of branches and twigs. The geese flew low to find this softer growth, ignoring the sandpipers, the godwits, the muskrats busy along the river banks.

And last the nest was lined with down from the goose's own body. Then she was ready to lay the eggs. The pair had flown all the long way north to lay the eggs and hatch the new goslings here on the shore of the arctic seas, under the long sunny skies of the arctic summer.

It was June and the goose was ready. On the brown island ringed with the still unmelted ice of winter, the mounded nest lay on the reedy, marshy land. Some distance away the gander waited as he had waited the other nine seasons of spring with his goose, waited for the laying of the eggs. This was only the beginning of the waiting for those would not be hatched until the end of the month. He would stand guard now and also during the other weeks until his mate was finished with the laying and the hatching. Then the family could move if necessary. Walking or swimming. The young would not be old enough to fly and the parent birds would not be able to fly, for at the end of the hatching came the season of molt. The great geese were earthbound then with the loss of their plumage. This extended the long season of waiting, until the new gray-brown feathers of the back and wings, the black of the tail and neck, and the soft gray of the underparts were grown anew. Then the season of waiting was ended!

But in this spring death would take the gander, and the goose would finish her waiting alone. Alone but for the goslings.

On a morning early in June the sun rose, warmer than the day before, bright after the short arctic night. Its rays slanted across the heath, silvering the fingers of the river, glancing from the ice pack out on the Beaufort Sea, marking the wide, wild landscape with the long shadows of dawn. In the narrow estuary between the small brown island and the land mass the ice of winter gave a sigh and settled into the silty water.

Now was the time for the goose. She squatted low on the soft cushion of the nest and the first egg was laid. It was a large egg, round, dull white. Inside the egg it was dark and warm, warm from the body of the goose. And the shadow of life within the egg responded to the warmth and grew.

Another egg was laid. And another. And another until there were seven within the nest, round and smooth and warm beneath the goose. Seven, but the first egg was the largest. The life within continued to grow. But one egg contained no shadow of life. The others were as they should be and the goose, covering them with her downy body, stretching her long neck flat across the surface and edge of the nest, was content now for the waiting.

And the gander stood his solitary guard away from the nest. Only once did he approach the goose on this day, to lay a tuft of grass beside her. She was not hungry. For a moment they laid their long necks together. The seasons had been good with them. Then the gander returned to his watch. The goose could see him there, his head high and straight above his strong body, the white cheek patches shining proudly in the June sunlight.

The twilight came and then the beginning of the short night. Within the largest egg the warm darkness continued unchanged, and the shadow of life was no longer so tenuous but a speck the size of a seed of grass. And it grew.

The next dawn too was clear, warmer still than the preceding one. Today the goose was hungry. The gander brought wild grasses and insects and once some small sour red berries that were good to her taste. She did not leave the eggs and the gander did not wander far in his search for food. The arctic summer was just beginning and though the food was not as plentiful as it would be in July, still there was enough and the gander had no difficulty in supplying his own and his mate's needs.

The days passed. The life within the large egg continued to grow, to expand. The seed grew until finally the shadowy shape of the gosling became defined. It gathered body and strength from the warm, dark sea around it.

The nights became shorter and finally past the middle of June the sun only rode low on the horizon and did not disappear. Now there would be no darkness at all for a while. But the large egg nestled deep in the nest beneath the downy breast of the goose, and within the egg there was no daytime.

Sometimes for the gander there was only the gathering of food to break the monotony of the long sunny hours, but it was not always easy and safe. A few days after the laying of the eggs the gander saw a mother wolf with two pups come along the far shore of the estuary. The she-wolf drifted as silent as a shadow but the pups rolled and bumbled along as though living were only a game and not to be taken seriously.

The old wolf knew better, for she must eat to nurse

her pups who were only partly weaned, and now she was hunting. She turned once and snarled softly at the young ones, and wisely they knew that the snarl was not part of their game and at least this must be taken seriously.

They disappeared beneath an outcropping of rock and the she-wolf was left free for her hunting. She had taken the scent of the geese on the island. Lifting her head, she scanned the opposite shore warily. Geese were not easy game. But they were good and fat now after the fortnight of feeding. If she had success, there would then be much milk for the pups and strength would return to her lean body. A floating log had jammed between the island and the bank on which the wolf stood. A bridge that would serve her purpose.

Across she started, belly low to the peeled white trunk of the driftwood log. Was this Death crawling silently toward the gander? *Not so soon, not so soon.* The goose would need him yet, for the time of the hatching was not here.

The wolf was halfway across the log. From the island came the trumpeting honk of the gander. Across the marshy ground to the end of the log the great bird rushed. His wings were stretched wide to their six-and-a-half-foot span, his long neck arched and the beak showed cruelly hard in the clear morning air. The feathers on his neck and body rose. Too late the she-wolf tried to whirl on the log for an ignominious retreat. But the log was narrow and slick from the washing waters and into the estuary tumbled the wolf. The mighty wings pummeled her, the sharp beak was everywhere at once. It was only by the greatest of fortune that she managed to struggle to the shore away from the island and pull herself half drowned under the cover of the brush.

Having routed the enemy, the gander had no desire to push the fight and he returned to his guard post on the island. From where he stood he could see the goose secure on her nest. This had not been the time for the parting.

Several times in his flights for food the gander saw men out on the ice pack, hunting the seals who lay sunning themselves and their pups. But this was far from the island. Twice the men came across the heath with some of their dogs, but even these did not approach the island too closely for the flats were still wet and boggy along the shore from the spring flood. Once with the men were several young ones, playing and talking and as heedless as the wolf pups had been. Three of the young ones were boys, but there was one girl, small and plump and laughing. She watched while the men shot or clubbed the rabbits or the ptarmigan and as with children of most hunting peoples the sight did not distress her, for they must eat and their dogs must eat. But twice when the young of the ptarmigan were left motherless she lingered behind and touched them lightly and said in a soft voice, "Poor baby ones." Nothing could be done for them though so she forgot about them and trudged sturdily after the men and the heedless boys.

The gander did not concern himself with the distant dangers but stayed close to the island where he could watch his mate patiently waiting, waiting on the eggs. Once a bear and her cub came swimming in the quiet current close to the island, but there was plenty for a bear to eat this time of year without fighting for it. So the cub and mother bypassed the little island when the gander spread his wings and gave his great racketing honk.

June drew to a close and July was at hand. The time for the hatching was near. And it was when the waiting was almost at an end that the shadow of Death became Death itself.

This last day of June on one of his flights for food, the gander had seen the men. They were far out on the heath, hunting, but there had been no cause for alarm. There were dogs and the plump girl-child, and three men. The girl was playing at following the hunting party. It was not far to the summer tents and she was able to take care of herself and find her own way in the wild country. Patiently her sturdy legs churned up and down as she followed the men and dogs, and it pleased her to think that she could trail the men without their knowing of it. When they stopped to make a kill or discuss some problem, she squatted in the low heath where they could not see her, covering her mouth with her hand to laugh silently, her dark eyes crescent moons of mirth. To think of her father and her two uncles, such great hunters, all unaware of being trailed by a girl-child!

From where she squatted in the brushy growth she twice saw the gander fly above them. He would have gone unnoticed by her except for his great size, but he was larger than any white-cheek she had seen. Perhaps because he was beautiful she formed a kind of attachment for him and watched to see him again. He did not come a third time. Finally she pretended to be the high-sailing gander, reaching her arms, tilting them this way and that in the cool arctic winds that brushed across the tundra from the Beaufort Sea.

She ran over the heath curving from side to side as she slanted her arms, toiling up the occasional hummocky rises to rush headlong down the other side, her round arms stretched evenly for the long glide, her body short and squat in the square garments. She was all sturdy solidity, but she could feel the grace of the big bird in her body. The Eskimo children were not brought up with a feeling for animals, but Mooshnuk was a rare one who responded to something inside of her that went even beyond the custom of her people.

While Mooshnuk played at flying, the gander gathered food for his goose. She was restless on her nest. The time for the hatching was here. Perhaps it was the faint stirrings within the eggs that made the goose rise stiffly and push at the pale spheres, turning them gently this way and that. The nervousness of the goose was passed to the gander, and his flights on this day grew shorter and finally he only hovered edgily between his guard post and the nest itself, making rough little burring sounds in his throat. It was on one of his excursions back to his guard post that he heard the voices of the men. He had taken little notice of them earlier when flying over the heath. Now suddenly his nervous fidgeting was over. He stood quietly on his mound looking away across the heath toward the west, toward the sound of the men.

The gander would not be with the flock when the Canada geese flew south at the end of summer. The goose would be alone except for the goslings, except for the young geese that by then would be flying. The gander would not see them fly. For those voices murmuring off in the distance but drawing closer, closer were the sound of Death.

The gander could see the men coming straight across the heath toward the shores of the estuary. The

land was no longer swampy along the shore, and floating debris had jammed against the log that the wolf
had tried to use. The bridge would be secure enough
for the men, a ready invitation. Another forty-eight
hours and the pair of geese with their goslings would
have been gone.

But still there was a little time. The gander turned
to look at his goose upon their nest. The sounds of the
voices had reached through her concern for the eggs
and now she was as quiet as her mate. She kept her
body low on the nest, but he could see her watching
him. Once more for the last time he went to her. He
poked softly at one of the pale eggs that rested beneath the down of her breast. It was the largest egg,
the one first laid at the beginning of June. He could
hear the stirring inside of the egg and a faint, a very
faint scrap of sound that was the gosling's voice. That
sound that was scarcely a sound at all would one day
clarion across the high northern sky when the great
honkers were flying!

The gander rustled the feathers of his back, his
wings. They were beginning to itch with the coming
molt. The voices on the land were closer. Now the
male ran his neck along that of his mate. For a moment they rested silently in that way. She uttered
only one low keening note. Now she must be silent
for the goslings.

The gander turned from the nest and walked down

to the tip of the island. He moved slowly along the spit of land until he reached the water's edge where the current folded softly around the downstream shore. There he slipped into the water, let the pull of it carry him fifty yards before he swam for the mainland bank.

He had left the island without flying, for the men might have seen him and after the kill have found the goose on the eggs. He had no way of knowing that the girl-child had outdistanced her elders and squatted in the heath atop a raised portion of the river bank. From there she had seen the goose and the nest. She saw the gander walk along the island and slip into the water. She saw him come to shore downstream. Mooshnuk knew from his size that it was the one she had seen sailing over the tundra, the one whose beauty she had felt within herself. She squatted there in the heath, and she could see the men and the dogs, and the island with the goose upon her nest. And the gander on the river bank where he stood tall and clear to view.

The men came across the heath toward the island. They walked steadily, stopping only when the dogs, excited over some wild smell, barked and ran in wide-ranging circles over the flat land. Mooshnuk sat quietly watching the drama below. When it was clear that the men would not miss the island if allowed to continue on their way, Mooshnuk saw the gander with a great flapping of wings rise into the air from the river bank. He swung in a circle over the tundra. The men and the dogs stopped walking and now their only movement was the slow turning of heads to watch the flight of the big bird. Once the gander lit for a moment and when he took to the air again he had a tuft of vegetation in his beak. Back he came and settled on the river bank, settled on the spot from which he had launched his circular flight.

He disappeared for a few moments and when he reappeared the stuff he had carried in his bill was gone. The men bent their track across the heath to meet the river where the gander was now standing guard. Of course, the gander was feeding his mate! They would find her on the nest along the river bank! A goose and a gander, good food for the cooking pot. The family would feast!

From her nest the goose could see the men coming, and the voices of the dogs grew louder. She stayed low, concealed by the reeds on the shore of their island. Far down the river bank she could see the tall standing neck of her mate with the white cheek patches proud in the sunlight, but she could feel the life beneath her, the tap-tapping within the largest egg, and she remained silent. As death was to be the lot of the gander so the silent watching was to be hers. And she kept her eyes on the gander until it was finished.

He did nothing to hide himself, nor did he seek

safety in flight. Instead he stood tall and as the dogs
drew near he ruffled his feathers and extended his
wings until he looked a giant of a bird defending his
home territory. The dogs lost some of the excited joy
from their running. Warily they circled to each side of
the bird. But the men came straight toward the gander.
They held their guns ready but perhaps if that one did
not take flight they could use a stick as a club and save
the precious ammunition. If the dogs could drag the
quarry to earth the stick would do. So the men
shouted, and the dogs rushed in from both sides.

The goose watched the bravery of her mate. He gave
no ground to the dogs but hissed and ran at them, the
powerful wings two dangerous flails that could break
the back of a dog, the beak a fast-moving spear. And it
was the dogs who gave ground. The men laughed at
this retreat, but then shouted angry commands to return to the battle.

Mooshnuk squatted unperturbed on the rise of the
river bank. Death was not new to her and even she
knew it was better to meet it bravely as the gander
was doing. It was necessary for some to die that others
might live in the hard life of the arctic.

The men's voices urged the dogs to their task.
Again the pack was driven back. And again. And
again. The men were amazed at the gander's fierce
bravery, but they shouted angrily at the dogs for each

retreat. Through eight charges the gander held his ground, once striking a dog such a blow across the hindquarters that that one did not return to the skirmish. He was tiring. The goose from her nest could see the uneven contest and the breath grew short within her own body as she watched.

On the ninth try one of the dogs, a powerful, squat, brown and white brute, came in low and made one slashing lunge at the neck of the gander. He missed, skidding from the thick down of the shoulder, grabbing at the wing as he fell. His teeth found a hold on the big humerus bone where it fitted into the shoulder socket, ground through the beautiful scapular and covert feathers there, and held to the bone in an unshakable grip. The good red blood of the gander gushed from the wound, dying the pale gray feathers of his breast. The life began to leave his body with the spread of the crimson stain.

With the bird held thus, the dogs lost their fear and rushed in for the kill. But now the men called them back. Food for the pot was best killed quickly and kept from the shredding teeth of the dogs. One man stepped forward, grasped the heavy stick firmly in his hand, raised it. The gander lifted his unbroken wing in one last act of defiance as the club descended. Once. Twice. And it was over.

The life of the gander flew from his body into the clear, cool arctic air.

The goose on her nest saw the great proud wing raised for that last time, and she saw the club descend. And as the club descended, she felt beneath her breast the cracking of that first, that largest egg.

As the old gander died, Chen was born.

2 Wolverine

It had been dark, dark. At first there had been endless space in the warm dark sea for the grain of life. But the grain grew, grew. And finally the hard dark confines of the once endless space closed close about the gosling. For the grain of life had become a gosling and the smooth, domed walls of his world would no longer contain him. Chen moved a little, at first feeling the walls just beyond the damp down of his body, but finally he could scarcely stir. The walls shrank in about him, his big feet were thrust up against his body, his head and neck were forced back along his side.

At last he could stand the pressure no longer. He must fight the confining walls, and he found that he had a weapon for them, a sharp, hard egg tooth. He started the attack. He worked furiously for a time, but the effort tired him and he rested. Again he started — peck, peck, peck, peck. The sound was loud around him, filling the dark world. He cried out from time to time and his new voice sounded mighty, giving strength to the movements of his neck and head as he worked.

Finally the egg tooth wore through a spot of the hard darkness, and there was light. A tiny diamond shard of light. As though this light made the remaining darkness even more unbearable Chen redoubled his effort. After mountainous labor the tiny jewels of light encircled the dark surface of his prison.

Now! Now! With a great convulsive movement of his body he thrust his cramped legs from him. The darkness burst apart! Chen lay blinking in the bright arctic light of the July morning.

With the light came sound. The silence of the egg was gone. Chen blinked at the light and was stunned by the sounds though he knew not what they were. Weakly he moved, then something hard, but with a gentleness, thrust him farther beneath the warm softness that spread above him. Here the light was less strong and the sounds were muffled. Muffled except for one sound, and this one had been with him even in the egg, even before the egg. It was the quick, steady, light sound of the goose's heart.

The gosling had no way of knowing that the loud sounds were the voices of the men and of the dogs. But instinctively he was frightened and his own scrap of heart fluttered fast and light, rocking him beneath his mother's breast. He crouched there silent, unmoving. There were other sounds. That of the arctic breeze in the rushes along the shore, the flow of the Mackenzie past the island, the cries of birds on distant bits of land.

There was no sound from the wolverine who crouched in the driftwood tangle at the upper end of this island. He, too, heard the voices of the men and the dogs and was silent. This was not wolverine territory, this open delta land of the great river. So he was cautious, silent in this foreign place. Bad luck had brought him here. He had been hunting, his quiet ferocious hunting, in a dry gully of one of the Mackenzie River tributaries. If he had known the reason for the dryness of the stream bed he would have hunted elsewhere. A quarter of a mile above him debris and mud had made a temporary dam that had blocked the flow of water from the spring breakup of the creek. The trapped waters had spread into a pond, the chunks of ice crowding it, melting slowly in the lengthening days until a small lake stood on the wooded flat above the earth dam, drowning the roots of the evergreens and the willows. Day by day the waters of the creek had collected, carrying debris that built the dam ever higher.

But the dam had no strength within itself and on the last morning of June with no warning at all it burst, and the force of the water sprang out with a rumbling roar on its way at last to the Beaufort Sea.

The wolverine hunted in the path of the roiling torrent. Too late he saw his danger. The wall of water towered above him, swept over him. Through a miracle he swam his way to the top but the force snatched him along with the trees and the sticks and the muddy debris. He managed to cling to one of the logs. Into the river the wolverine and the log plunged and the strength of the flood thrust them into the main current. It had been a long voyage and finally the wolverine had dragged his short-legged, powerful body to the shelter of the little island.

When the men were gone he would make a kill, eat, reach the shore and start the trek back to his forest country.

Chen knew nothing of the noisy men, nor the silent wolverine. Nor did he know of Mooshnuk squatting stolidly on the rise of the river bank, crouched on the brown heath, watching the men and the dogs as they searched for the nest of the goose. The gander had done his last job faithfully and well. The men and dogs did not think of the island, but searched the bank near where the kill had been made, slowly working their way farther and farther from the island. The fear eased in the heart of the goose.

Mooshnuk arose, watched the men for a little longer. She could see the body of the gander as one of the men carried it slung over his shoulder. The beautiful body was limp, thumping lifeless against the man, the wings dragged down by their own weight, never to fly again. Suddenly Mooshnuk felt a terrible sadness that she had never felt before at a kill. The men had killed more than a gander.

The girl raised her arms, arching them in a wing curve. She ran a dozen steps down the slant of the land, tilting from side to side. But the joy was gone. She dropped her arms to her side and walked slowly to the flat shore. The gander had given her heart freedom and beauty. Now she was earthbound again.

She stood beside the estuary looking across at the island. From here it was difficult to see the nest of the goose. Mooshnuk was turning away when the log caught her attention. Going back to the log she pushed at it with one foot, found it solid, and without knowing exactly why crossed to the island. Along the shore the reeds were thick but when she had pushed through the rushy barrier Mooshnuk could see the rough nest and the bird upon it. The goose was suddenly aware of this new danger and with no gander to protect her and the hatching goslings she must do what she could herself. On the mound of the nest she hissed and ruffled her feathers, spreading her wings to frighten the girl-child away.

"I only want to look," Mooshnuk explained softly as though the bird would understand.

This was a small human thing with no dogs and no stick, and the sound of the voice puzzled the goose. Her feathers settled a little and she stopped the hissed warning for a moment to inspect this intruder.

"There, you see? I mean no harm to you." Mooshnuk moved closer to the nest and now there was much of the island between her and the shore. She had no way of knowing of the danger that crept down from the upper tip of the island along the water's edge. Neither she nor the goose could sense the presence of the wolverine, but the breeze blowing upriver had carried the scent of both to the silent ferocious animal. He moved down among the reeds beside the log. His always-angry eyes glared at Mooshnuk's sturdy back as she moved slowly toward the nest; beyond the girl the wolverine could see the goose. Today his luck was good. The human was small and would be of little danger, though a grown human the wolverine would avoid. And the goose would be good eating, with perhaps eggs or a few goslings in the nest. But for the time being the wolverine only hid and watched.

Mooshnuk knew the goose would not let her come
to the nest, but she had a curiosity to see at least one of
the goslings. It would be a young one of the gander,
the beautiful gander that flapped dead and flightless
now against the back of one of the men. Yes, she really
wanted to see the gander's young.

"Let me see only one, mate of that beautiful gander
who called in the skies," she pleaded moving step by
step closer to the nest.

The goose was frightened, but confusion was with
the fright for she could see the girl-child and beyond
the girl in the reeds beside the log was the dark
shadow of the wolverine. If only the goslings were
hatched and she did not have to stay tied to the danger
of this open spot! She could feel another of the eggs
hatch and the movement of the damp baby one beneath her. By tomorrow they could leave the nest for
the safety of the water and the reedy shores. Now she
must protect the young ones from the small human
and the terror of the wolverine.

Mooshnuk moved one step nearer and knew when
the goose arose, standing tall on the mound of the
sticks and twigs, that she could draw no closer. But
this was close enough! For there beneath the goose
she could see the young ones.

"Five!" she said softly, careful not to move lest the
frightened goose should fly at her. She remembered

the howl of the dog when the gander beat it with his great wings, and she stood very still. "Five, and two yet to hatch." For she had no way of knowing that one of the eggs had no life.

The goose did not fly at Mooshnuk, but remained poised over the eggs. The shadow had moved from the cover of the reeds along the shore. Hunger drove the wolverine. Now he must make his kill and eat.

Chen had been out of the egg long enough for the down to dry on his body, and strength to come to his legs. The other goslings were either drying or more recently dried than Chen and none had the curiosity of that first and largest gosling. He struggled in the softness of the down-lined center of the nest until he could reach the rough twiggy rim. There he teetered, facing the world, with the goose's great body towering above him.

And Mooshnuk, all unaware of her danger, laughed aloud at the small Chen. She only let her voice move, holding her body still so the goose would stay on the nest.

"What a bold small one you are! Your father's spirit flew into your body. You are brave and bold and you shall fly with beauty."

Mooshnuk now carefully began to back away from the nest. She had seen what she had come to see and now she would leave the goose and her goslings in peace. Still moving carefully, slowly she turned to make her way to the edge of the island, to the log bridge.

And she stopped and did not move and her voice was silent now. The breeze stopped and everything in the broad arctic land beneath the high pale cloudless sky seemed frozen. Only the river made its soft sound along the shore as Mooshnuk stood facing the wolverine. She had never seen an animal such as this. But from her memory came the stories that were told around the fire in the long dark night of winter. Travelers from the forest regions had told of this one, this animal hated and feared by the Eskimos of the forest lands. This wolverine.

She had heard of how in winter the wolverine would hunt the big caribou, then leap upon the shoulders of the luckless one, holding with powerful jaws, grinding, grinding, until the sharp teeth found the spine and snapped it, and the caribou's shaking and running had been for nothing for there it would lie dead in the snow. And the lonely-running wolverine would eat a little and then be off. Lonely he was, for he did not want to be with even his own kind.

Mooshnuk stood without moving and all the world seemed to have stopped. She knew the ways of the wild, and looking into the eyes of the wolverine she knew that with her first movement now he would make his charge, his short-legged, spraddled, powerful charge.

Without turning her head she looked about. Her dark eyes searched for a way of escape, but she did not let her mind fly apart with panic. She remembered the gander and how he had fought with his mind and his heart. And she did not let the panic rule her.

The men were long since gone. There was no one to help her but herself. A weapon. If only she had a weapon. A weapon to stand between herself and those terrible jaws. Still without moving she looked from side to side. She was aware that the wolverine shifted. His broad brown body, nearly a yard in length, tensed. His sharp little ears slanted back along his skull. The dark muzzle wrinkled, pulling the lips back from the hungry fangs.

The only thing Mooshnuk could see was a thick jagged branch of driftwood. It was jammed upright into the sandy soil of the island. It had been left when the first of the spring flood swept over this spot.

The branch was between her and the wolverine. She would have to run directly toward the animal to reach it. All of her body wanted to run away. But her mind and her heart were brave. Before the animal could start his charge the girl rushed forward. In doing so she caught the beast unawares. He was only famil- iar with fleeing things. His hesitation lasted only for

a moment. And in that moment Mooshnuk reached
the branch, wrenched it from the sandy soil, flung it
up before her. In the same instant the wolverine
launched himself through the air.

The broken jagged end of the branch was in his
face before he saw it. It rammed into the ugly open,
fang-rimmed mouth. Mooshnuk's short solid body
had braced itself in the act of using the weapon and
the full weight of the wolverine thrust the stick down
his throat. With a howl of agony and surprise the
animal wrenched himself free, blood pouring from
his mouth. He coughed painfully several times, then
turned, and snarling over his shoulder, disappeared
into the rushes.

With the danger past, Mooshnuk was weak. Her
legs would scarcely stand, and her hands found difficulty in grasping the stick, now red with the wolverine's blood. But after a moment she forced herself
to follow the animal's trail. Just within the shelter of
the reeds she found the sandy earth widely stained
with blood. She knew that the wolverine would not
be back soon. Perhaps never.

Chen had watched from his perch on the rim of the
nest. His down was soft and dry, but he was trem-
bling. Within the egg there had been only himself.
This new world was full of light and noise and vio-
lence. He clung there to the twiggy rim with his
mother towering gray and strong above him.

He called the mighty call he had used within the egg, but it was lost in this new world. Mooshnuk heard the scrap of sound and turned to look at the nest. Despite her recent terror she now laughed a soft laugh.

"Oh, small gosling! Someday you will make the skies ring as your father once did. Today I saved not only myself from the wolverine. May you live to sail the skies in beauty!"

Chen called out a defying cry to the world, looked boldly at the laughing girl, watched as she turned and started across the log. On the far side of the estuary she faced about and now solemnly raised one arm in a farewell salute. Chen still watched as she finally turned her back to the river and made her solid, steady way across the brown tundra, her figure growing smaller and smaller until she was swallowed by the bigness of the land.

The goose picked up the boldest, the biggest of her brood and thrust him back into the safety of the nest. Chen squawked his protest but the air was chill with the sun swinging low on its arc, so he settled comfortably beneath the body of his mother. There were others like himself now within the nest and they burrowed and scurried about in the soft semi-darkness of the goose's down, making small gosling noises to one another. Their world here seemed as safe as within the egg, and they were content for the moment.

The goose was getting hungry without her mate to feed her. Impatiently she waited for the last egg. When it hatched she would take the goslings to the river's edge and the hunger would be over and done with, for the arctic was generous with her wild ones in the month of July. The hunger would be gone and gone too the helpless danger she was exposed to here on the nest.

But for Chen there was no danger. After that brief fear when first he had emerged from the egg, the world had seemed wonderful and secure. And exciting. He nudged his siblings. He stretched his body and his small wings, and tramped about in the downy cup of the nest. He bumped against the last egg, but its quiet smoothness remained undisturbed. He reached high into the down of his mother's body and could not reach through the depth of its softness. He called aloud and again his voice was mighty trapped in the confines of the nest beneath the goose. He did all of these things and did them again. And again. And again.

And all the time his body grew in strength, readying the gosling to face the world of the river, the rushes, the tundra. He knew nothing of the dangers that awaited there in the black waters of the Mackenzie, there in the tangle of the reeds and rushes, there in the thatch of the heath. He knew nothing of life and therefore knew nothing of death.

But the old goose shifted restlessly, several times arising to poke at the tardy egg. She did not know it would never hatch. So the useless waiting held her there and the risk was great for her and for the goslings.

In the thickest growth of the rushes where the water ran softly along the edge of the island the wolverine lay with the pink froth of blood edging the dark muzzle. He had watched Mooshnuk depart while the agony burned in his throat, while the hot blood filled his mouth. He had watched her leave and lay quietly with the weakness of his wound. Finally the bleeding had lessened and the pain was not so fierce. As the torture of the wound subsided, the torture of his empty belly increased. His hunger had returned. The saliva flowed, mingling with the pink froth, and the wolverine painfully licked with his hungry tongue. But the weakness would not let him rise, so he waited.

And on the nest the goose waited for the last egg to hatch.

The sun swung to its lowest point and then began its shallow, slow climb of the arctic sky, and thus the night was passed again with no darkness. The goose was restless upon the nest. The goslings were hungry. They could not wait much longer for their venture into the world beyond the nest. Yet she was loath to leave the last egg unhatched. She turned it once more and tapped it lightly with her beak. It was silent. But Chen and the other downy ones were not silent as they scrabbled restlessly, hungrily about her carefully stepping feet.

Chen himself was the noisiest, the boldest. He struggled from the soft center of the nest to the harsh rim. There he teetered, bravely facing the gentle morning breeze, valiantly flapping his small wings for balance. He voiced his call of defiance to the wind, and though it was a greater sound than the one at which Mooshnuk had laughed it did nothing to crease the silence of the great land and of the sky.

The goose made her decision. The last egg must be left unhatched. Carefully, lest she tread on one of the buff downy babes, she made her way from the nest. As she moved, three of the long primary feathers of her wings loosened and were left in the nest. The molt had begun.

She called softly to the goslings. There was an urgency in her voice. The pressure of danger was upon her and she called again to her aimless young. Chen did not wait for another call. He was tired of the nest, and he was hungry. He tottered from twig to twig over the wide roughness of the rim. Near the edge he caught one awkward foot. It was an endless fall to the ground. He stood up, called angrily, hoarsely in his gosling voice, shook his down with a ruffling of his little wings, then strutted boldly forth until he stood under the shadow of the goose's body.

Perhaps, in the end, it was really Chen who saved them from the wolverine, for on seeing Chen's success (and who was there to say that falling was not the proper way to leave the nest) the other goslings trooped forth in single file, staggering, teetering across the rim, making their own individual ignominious descents to the flat sand of the island. The goose with nervous urgings started across the land toward the estuary. In other years the gander had led them and she had protected the last baby from the rear. But this year she was alone.

She looked behind her every few steps to check on stragglers, but her small downy regiment marched bravely at her heels, single file, doughty, all unaware of the dangers of this, their first day. For the first-day loss of goslings in the arctic lands is great and only the hardy and the lucky survive.

If the gander had been with them they would have stopped to eat. But the goose dared not stop in this open spot. And it was fortunate for her and for the goslings that she did not.

In the thick growth of the reeds the wolverine stirred. The bleeding had stopped and some of the strength had returned to his body. If he was to live he must find food. He stood and found his legs solid beneath him. Softly he started down the length of the island. He had seen the goose and she had looked fat to him in his hunger. The saliva ran in his mouth and his eyes were sharp and glistening at the thought of the feast.

But carefully, carefully. He had no desire to meet that girl-child, that one with the stick. The goose had forgotten the wolverine. Now she watched for the danger from the sky; watched for the glaucous gull whose swoop and cruel beak could snatch a gosling in a flick of time; watched for the jaeger who would steal a lone stray downy one; watched for the silent, swift white death that rode the wings of the snowy owl.

Chen tramped at her heels, raising his big webbed feet, placing them with solemn awkward care in the crisp grasses, on the pebbly roughnesses of his great new world. He did not know of danger. The other goslings came close behind, all but the last, who became entranced with a bright beetle that crawled before him. That one was left behind as his brothers and sisters marched on. There had come the faintest of sounds from the brush. The goose without her gander could not watch in all directions at once. She swung her head about to stare at the screening brush as she caught the first warnings of danger from the wolverine. The shadow of an owl's wings swept over them and the last loitering gosling was snatched away by cruel talons with no more than its small shriek of terror to mark its passing.

The five remaining goslings now seemed to sense

that thing called danger and jostled and pushed at one another, rushing for the protecting body of the goose. Perhaps it was the loss of the one that saved the five, for the goose had now taken alarm. Her voice, her bill, her wings urged, swept her brood to the water's edge. Not thirty feet away the brush shook, parted. Out thrust the ugly head of the wolverine. The goose had stepped into the shallows leading the way for her babies, who now teetered at the edge of the strange blue-gray stuff that moved past the solid land. The peremptory cry of the old bird reached Chen. He had led the others from the nest; now he responded to his mother's call and launched himself into the stream. There he bobbed like a buff-colored cork.

The other four goslings popped into the water after Chen. Another instant of hesitation and the wolverine's rush would have caught them. The beast's jaws snapped only on thin air. Mother and babes swept away downstream on the quick current and were soon lost to sight in the rushes.

The wolverine prowled the shore with rage in his heart and hunger in his belly.

3   Earthbound

Chen moved his big feet in the wonderful water; he squawked at the sky and the reeds and the river; he gabbled to the goose and to the other goslings. The world was only delight! Gone was the darkness of the egg. Danger had been only a shadow. With no teaching he upped his little tail to the sky, thrusting his head into the cool green world of water. What delicate bulbs for the eating, what tender aquatic plants, what luscious scooting bugs! Of such things is made the magic of growth.

But the goose was wise. Never is danger past. To forget for only an instant invites disaster. Now she watched the sky and also constantly arched her long neck to peer into the river depths for the pike whose gray-green form, like the shadow of death, could snatch a gosling below the surface of the water never to return to the world of sunshine and light and air. But as she watched, the goose talked all the while with her babes, her voice soft and lisping and scarcely to be heard by other than the five bobbing downy blobs.

Of the five there were three males with Chen the largest of all. The two female goslings were timid and swam close to the old goose. Chen was bold but even in this first day of his life the wisdom of the gander was stirring in his head. Through some instinct his bright black eyes took in all around him and he was wary of all movement except the natural flow of the water. Thus when the surface was roiled from below he thrust himself away from the spot with quick feet. Not so a brother equally bold but not equally wary. And in that way the second gosling was snatched away. The cruel jaws of a pike pulled the gosling out of sight. There was only the treacherous swirl of the water for that one instant and it was over.

Now the goose had only the four left. But with each passing hour the small ones became more aware of their world, more cautious, yet more skilled in swimming. When their mother led them ashore on the main body of land, they stayed close to her protecting body. The first day passed and the second, and the remaining goslings survived.

By the end of the second week the seeds, the sprouts of tundra growth, the river plants, the bugs and crawling things, the crowberries had wrought their magic. The goslings were no longer tiny balls of fluff. Their round bodies had grown long, the wings strengthened though the flight feathers would not show for some time. They were still buff, but the down was darkened with the promise of feathers along wing and tail edges. Wisdom had increased with each day of passing time. No longer did the old goose have to be the only eyes for this family flock. Now all watched for danger. And already Chen was a leader. Both his size and his wisdom had grown beyond that of his brother and sisters.

Mooshnuk came several times to sit silently on some hummocky rise beside the river. She saw the goose and her four young ones. The girl knew that this would be the family of the dead gander, and she knew the largest of the young was that one who had climbed to the edge of the nest on that first day and thrown his scrap of voice at the world. When she thought of how he would soon sail high and far, his wondrous wild voice sounding across the great empty curve of the sky, she would laugh and then rise to her feet and run down the slant of the land, stretching her short, sturdy arms to the side and tilting in earthbound flight. The gander's beauty had not died beneath the hunter's club. It would live again in Chen.

The goose was at the height of her molt. She and her young were earthbound. Her new plumage and the first plumage of the goslings began to appear, and the geese spent much time in the sunny endless days preening and picking at themselves, perhaps to relieve the itching, perhaps to hurry the growth so the flightless days would be over. This was the time of great danger, for the only way to escape their enemies was by swimming or hiding. So even as they preened or searched for food they watched.

The goslings grew until they were no longer goslings. Babyhood is short for the wild creatures. Chen himself was beginning to stand tall; his neck had become longer, graceful and flexible; his wings strong. Already he was testing them against the winds, pushing high on reaching legs, thrusting himself tall, taller, standing on only the tips of his webbed feet, beating, beating the strengthening pinions until they made a muffled whirr.

No longer was there fear of the glaucous gull, the snowy owl, or the great eagles who drifted high in the empty upper air on tireless wings. No pike would dare snatch at the paddling feet, now grown so large. With

effortless ease those feet thrust the great gray forms
across the roof of the pike's watery domain.

But the greatest danger of all to the geese increased
as they grew larger. Goslings would be of little use
over the Eskimos' cooking fire, but ah, a goose, a large
young goose, that was different.

The wolves, the solitary roaming wolves, or the
mated pairs with their half-grown young, were a danger. And the wolverine. Had that one filled with hunger returned to the forest lands?

But still even the young geese knew that it was man
who was the greatest enemy.

Occasionally hunting parties came across the tundra but always the old goose was wary and she would
see the danger before it came too close. Then she
warned her young ones in the soft lisping sound that
carried only far enough to reach the most distant
wanderer. In that instant all the tall standing heads
would drop close to the ground, and thus obscured by
the low growth, they would scurry away to slip into
the waters of the Mackenzie and disappear along the
reedy shores.

Whenever she could leave the family tents, Mooshnuk came across the wide land to the river. Never had
she cared about the hunting before. The men's kill
of the day had only been of interest in that it filled the
cooking pot. Now each time she came to the river she
prayed that her young gander would have discovered

the magic of flight. For only in flight was there safety.

"Will you never fly, son of that great one who sailed the skies?" she asked aloud one day. Perched upon a knoll that overlooked the fanned delta land, she spoke only to herself and the empty arctic wind.

There was exasperation in her voice, concern in her eyes. These geese must surely be learning their lessons more slowly than she learned her own! Her dark eyes sparkled with laughter. To think the young geese could be as reluctant to fly as she to learn reading and writing at the government school! But even with reluctance she had learned, so surely the white-cheeks who now constantly beat at the air with eager wings would soon be earthbound no longer.

"Soon you must fly, you lovely gander, and someday you will be as mighty as your father. The days grow short and cool, and the nights long and chill. The time of flying *must* be soon. If only the hunters —"

And the words she spoke only for her own ears stopped. With apprehension she glanced across the heath. There had come the sound of men's voices, carried from a distance by a capricious current of air. Only for a moment she heard them, then there was silence again except for the birds' voices in the tundra growth and over the water and along the reedy shores and islands.

It was then that she saw the goose and her four

young ones. Ah, the men were far away and there were a thousand directions they could go. That goose and her young were surely safe for now.

"Oh, you lovely ones," she whispered. "You brave, lovely birds. Perhaps today you will fly and I shall see you. Then my heart will travel the skies also."

And indeed this was the day! The new plumage of the old goose was glossy in the sun. When she stretched her wings the long primary feathers showed tight and unblemished with no tears in the wonder of their webbing. The soft shorter feathers of her body and breast held sleek and smooth over the thick light down beneath. The black of her head and neck was set off by the shining white patch stretching beneath her neck and high on either cheek. And miraculously the once small and downy young now could be distinguished from the parent bird only by their lesser size. But Chen, ah Chen, he had grown almost as large as the old goose herself.

Now as Mooshnuk watched, the goose spread her wings, sailed low over the tundra and in a circle back to her watching, wondering young. The girl could hear the excited gabbling and clacking of the goose and Chen and the others. Silently she laughed to herself. Those birds were as full of talk as her own people when they gathered at the post store in Aklavik.

Presently the old goose sailed in her circular flight once more. Chen had watched the goose's first flight with motionless attention. At this second flight now, he called his loud *hauk-hauk*, then ran rapidly across the ground after the sailing goose, reaching his wings far on each side of his body. The goose circled and Chen turned, ran back as she landed beside the others.

In excitement he again gave his loud hauk-hauking cry. When the goose rose into the air for the third time, Chen began his run once more, and now the other three young geese followed behind him. This time, though, when Chen reached his wings wide he beat them against the arctic breeze. In his terrible urge to leave the slow ground, his pinions thrust faster, faster. *Hauk-hauk*, he called! In desperation the wings moved with ever greater speed. Finally in a fury of effort he thrust the earth away from him with a kick of his big feet.

The miracle! The wondrous miracle! For each bird that flies the miracle must happen. One moment earthbound, the next with wings and wind and will the miracle is performed. The sky is theirs! And so it was with Chen.

The heavy pull that had chained him to the earth suddenly released him. The ground fell away, the voices of his siblings receded. The things of earth ceased to exist. There were only the sky and the air, the wonderful moving currents of pure cold air that thrust upward beneath his wings carrying him aloft; the air, unseen, but as real, as strongly felt as the flow-

ing waters of the Mackenzie. Chen stopped the beating of his wings. He rested lightly on the air, rocking
unsteadily in the newness of flight, tilting this way
and that, finding the tail feathers could steady him.
Above the tundra he glided.

And below on the top of a hummock a girl-child
stood upright. Her laugh echoed the triumph of the
young gander's *hauk-hauk*. Her sturdy legs carried her
a few steps down the hill. She tilted her stubby arms
from side to side, then stopped to gaze upward. Her
body was earthbound but her heart flew in the currents of the upper air.

She had forgotten the hunters. For Chen there was
no wariness in this moment, only the wonder of flight.
The other three young geese had not yet shed the
shackles of earth. But they had forgotten all else in
their effort. Only the old goose was suddenly aware of
the danger that had drawn close. Too close! She gave
her quick cry of warning. Her circle closed in a tight
spiral and she was with her three earthbound young.

Chen heard his mother's cry, but the wind beneath
his wings swept him along. He did not know how to
return to the others. When he turned his head to scan
what lay below, he saw that his flight had not carried
him high from the earth. But his mother, his brother,
his sisters were nowhere in sight. Instead there were
three strange creatures no more than a willow's height
below him. The strange ones each carried a stick. As

Chen looked, one of them pointed its stick into the air. There was a loud boom crashing through the silence. Then for an instant odd whistling flicks of sound were in the air around him. There was scarcely time for fright before the booming sound came again. This time a hot pain burned across Chen's right wing. The buoying air dropped from under him. He was toppling toward the ground. His wings flapped uselessly. There was the crash of breaking twigs, a thud as his body dropped through the screening growth to the ground. He lay stunned for a breath of time.

Chen stirred when he heard the men's voices, felt through the ground the tread of their feet. Through the lacework of the branches above and around him he could see the arch of the sky, the rise of a hummock of ground. His injured wing was hot with pain but he was able to pull it in against his side. Without a sound and thrusting his long neck straight before him he moved away from the spot where he had fallen. Some of his blood had stained the ground there, but now with the wing against him, the down of his body sheltered the wound and there was no trail of red to mark his passage. Was the old gander's wisdom stirring in his head, the old one's courage who had died defending his mate and their young? Chen moved low through the tundra growth, scarcely touching the close branches. There was no sound, no waving of brush to betray him.

At the first cry of the goose when she had seen the danger, Mooshnuk on her hummock had pressed her hands to her mouth, then stood unmoving, her dark eyes round with fear for the young gander. Surely, surely this one must not die in the same season as had his father! If the men of her family killed this one, Mooshnuk felt that the wonderful soaring beauty which had filled her own body would die also. Her heart would become as gray, as cold, as bleak as the stones beside the arctic sea.

From the hummock Mooshnuk had seen Chen when he fell. She watched and saw him stir. Her heart beat again when he managed to stand, but she caught her lip between her teeth as the gander with difficulty drew his injured wing to his body. With wonder she saw his stealth as he crept low through the tundra growth. Ah, the wise brave young one!

When the men came to the spot and saw the blood upon the ground they spoke quickly to one another and searched for some sign of the bird.

"They must not find him," Mooshnuk whispered to the wind. Then she called to the men, "The bird you shot fell where you stand, but he has crept off. I saw him once in that spot over where the brush is thin and then his head showed even beyond."

She thrust one arm out pointing the direction for the men to follow. Her cheeks flushed at the lie and she was glad her father was at a distance and could not look into her eyes.

"It is Mooshnuk," her father, Akshuya, said to the other two. Then he called to her, "That far? The white-cheek could move that fast though hurt by my shot?"

"He seemed only stunned," she answered. "Much luck in your hunting! A young goose for the cooking pot will please my mother. And your belly!"

Shame for this deception filled her, but she was frantic with fear that the men would find the gander.

Akshuya laughed and raised one hand. "If our hunting is good you shall have the liver for your help, Mooshnuk!"

She tried to laugh, but could not. Then the men turned and moved off across the tundra in the direction she had shown.

"The beautiful one will not be for the cooking pot this night," Mooshnuk whispered. She watched the men for a moment, swallowing at the lump in her throat that her fear and the lie had made. Finally she moved to the far side of the hummock where they could no longer see her and anxiously scanned the heath below. She wanted to go down and look for the wounded bird but she dared not until the men had given up their search and gone on for further hunting.

Chen had moved as rapidly as he dared though the

pain in his wing was a fierce fire. He had never been separated from the family flock before. The urge to find them forced him on and presently he could hear the sound of the Mackenzie.

There was a weakness within him and he wanted to call and hear the old goose answer. Yet he dared not. The weakness forced him to stop. Now he let the injured wing droop. The pellets had torn the feathers and the flesh of the leading edge of his right wing near the body. Only luck had saved his life. On that first time aloft his wavering, tilting flight had tipped him out of the hunter's line of fire or the shot would have entered his breast.

Blood from the wing stained Chen's feathers; he hunched in the brush, his breathing fast and light from the weakness, his black eyes glazed. It was thus that Mooshnuk found him when the men had finally given up the search and gone. Chen did not hear her approach for the weakness still held him. When he saw her he only hissed a little. Did some memory stir within him of that first day when he had stood on the edge of the nest and she had not harmed him, but had spoken softly and then turned to face the wolverine? Perhaps not. Perhaps it was only the weakness that kept him for the moment passive, unmoving.

"Ah, poor lovely bird," Mooshnuk said softly. She moved a little closer to peer at the wound. "It is bleeding, but it does not look as though the wing is broken."

Chen hissed again, but he did not move. Mooshnuk backed away a little, frowning in thought. After a moment she whispered, "You white-cheek, stay in this spot and I shall return and poultice your wing."

She moved off quickly toward the sound of the water. At the river's edge she searched along the bank until she found a certain low-growing gray-green plant. She pinched off a bit and smelled it. Now she gathered more and searched yet farther for a spot where she could scoop a handful of mud from beside the flowing water. She worked the mud and the aromatic plant into a soft ball, then turned and started back the way she had come. Pausing then, she went back to the water.

"He will be thirsty with his wound," she said to herself. Finding an old log, peeling and wet, she pried a small sheet of bark loose, furled it into a rude cup, filled it with water.

In a few minutes she was back beside the dazed gander. Moving slowly, Mooshnuk held the water where Chen could reach it. He hissed softly, but as the girl held the bark cup without moving, the gander's thirst overcame his fear. Warily watching, he stretched his long neck forward and touched the water with his bill. All seemed safe. He scooped up some of the liquid and tilted his head so the coolness could run down his throat. The one swallow seemed to bring him strength and courage. He dipped again and again until the water was gone. Now he started to rise but the girl's voice held him and he hissed again, uneasily. Still, that strange young one had not hurt him and the water had been good.

Perhaps she meant no harm and the soft sound of her voice was pleasant. Chen stopped his hissing and watched with bright wise eyes. She still stooped unmoving before him, talking, softly talking all the while. After a bit she reached one hand slowly toward him. Chen shifted, but the weakness still held him so he did not arise. When Mooshnuk touched him lightly on the wing near the burning wound he turned his head on its long flexible neck, drew it back, then thrust forward with his hard beak. The girl did not flinch nor pull her hand away, nor did she stop the soft talking. Chen stopped the thrust of his beak just short of her hand and once more turned his bright gaze upon her.

"You are a wise bird," she continued softly. "I only wish to help and the bleeding of your wing has not stopped yet. But luck was with you for the bone is unbroken. Ah, what a terrible thing if that great bone had been shattered. That one short flight would have been the last —" And her quiet voice went on and on while slowly, slowly her hand moved along the wing.

Geese always talk greatly when flocked together. Perhaps that was why the girl's speaking quieted him though he trembled under the touch of her hand. Once or twice he hissed again but several times he made a little churring, gabbling sound in his throat.

"Ah, we are speaking to one another. I say my words and you the words of a white-cheek. I cannot understand, though some sound a little like those of a lowly snake and the rest like *chen-chen-chen* —"

Mooshnuk cared not what she said but only continued talking to calm the gander. Seeming scarcely to move her fingers, she slipped them below Chen's wing and lifted very gently. Once more he made the motion to strike her with his powerful beak; once more he stopped the blow before it landed.

Now she moved her other hand forward. In this hand was the soft mud and herb. Her legs hurt from the long stooping and she tried to keep her hand from shaking with the strain of the slow movement and the awkward position. She blinked with concentration. And she continued the soothing chatter.

"Ah, *chen-chen-chen*, you are a good bird, *chen-chen-chen*, raise your wing a little, *chen-chen-chen*, you are brave like your father, now the poultice, *chen-chen-chen*, do not strike me with that strong beak, you *chen-chen-chen*. Ah, this will stop the burning and the bleeding —"

And with a long, smooth, gentle movement she spread the cool, clinging mud over the wound. It stayed like a new skin. The bleeding was stopped. With the raw surface closed from the air the burning was gone. Only the weakness remained and this was a good thing for it held Chen quiet.

"There." Mooshnuk breathed a sigh and sat back upon the ground. In this position the gander's head was higher than her own. She looked up at him and her brown eyes shone as she laughed softly. "You *chen-chen-chen,* perhaps you will fly the skies after all."

The gander made the churring, gabbling sound again.

"You must have a name, oh friend of mine. You have named yourself! Chen. Yes, Chen I shall call you." She stood up then and moved a little back. She had forgotten and her movement was sudden. For a moment the gander was startled and rose unsteadily to his feet.

"Ah, I am sorry I frightened you. Poor Chen with your injured wing," Mooshnuk said. An idea came to her mind as she saw the gander standing thus. He would fly away to the south in a few weeks. If he returned in the spring to this nesting ground would she recognize him? She felt in her pockets and found nothing that would suit her purpose. Next she inspected the bracelet on her arm. It was of metal and would do. Slipping off the bracelet, she bent one end back and forth, back and forth. It took several minutes to fashion the narrow flexible strip of the size she wanted. Next she took a knife from the roomy pocket of her loose garment and laboriously scratched at the metal.

"That learning of letters and words at the school is of some use after all," she thought, smiling a little as she looked at the completed job.

There were two words scratched into the metal. CHEN and, in smaller letters, AKLAVIK. The last was the small town where Mooshnuk went to school during the long dark winter when her family left their summer tents on the edge of the Beaufort Sea and returned to their home in Aklavik.

Moving slowly again so Chen would not take flight, with some difficulty Mooshnuk managed to fasten the metal band securely — not too tight, not too loose — about the leg of the gander. Twice Chen hissed and once made the striking motion with his beak, but he did not hurt that one who had stopped the pain in his wing.

At last the girl stood up. "I have seen bands on a few of the birds killed and brought for the cooking pots. My father says it marks where the birds are from and he gives the bands to the man at the post in Aklavik. At least I shall know you next spring if you return, you lovely brave Chen."

With no further words now Mooshnuk backed away and moved out across the tundra. After two dozen steps she looked back. The gander was no longer in sight. He would be safely hidden there until the weakness left him.

4   Thousands of Geese

The old goose and the three young ones gave excited little cries and talked much in their soft lisping way when at last they found Chen. He was still hunched beneath the tundra brush, but slowly his strength returned. Finally, with the goose making coaxing sounds, he stood up and after a bit they all moved off in the direction of the river.

Chen's wing ached. He held it to him and moved stiffly along. There would be no flying today, nor tomorrow, nor the next. The instinct for flight stirred within him and he stretched his neck and gave an impatient cry. His pain stilled the boldness though, and at the water's edge he followed the others, gently easing himself into the water to glide out away from the dangers of the land, to move through the safe rushes. The five of them ate and gabbled. Only the old goose rose into the air a few times to try the joy of her returned flight.

Chen did not dive, nor did he stretch the injured wing for some time, and Mooshnuk's healing poultice had done its good work before the mud cracked and was washed away by the water.

While the goslings had grown and become geese, the land had changed from spring to summer. But the season of warmth and growth is short in the arctic. The ever-shining sun of June and July now slid below the horizon each day. By the middle of August the nights were dark and cold. The ponds and some of the narrow still inlets of the Mackenzie froze each night, only to thaw in the day with the faint warmth of the low-riding sun. As the days passed the open water of the Beaufort Sea that lay black between the eternal ice pack and the rocky shore became marked with occasional skim ice that gradually clotted into unstable islands. These in turn were pushed together by the winds and cemented by the freezing nights. In this way the everlasting polar ice extended itself to the south, gradually narrowing the black strip of the sea.

Many of the birds of arctic Canada had left for warmer climes by the middle of August. Most of the shore birds were gone; no longer did the raucous voices of gulls sound along the rocky coast; gone were the dunlin, the ringed plover, the sanderling.

By this third week in August the old goose was fully through with her molt. She was restless and this restlessness increased with each day. The time of migration was near.

Chen's two sisters and his brother were now able to rise from water or ground with a great flapping of wings and they sailed over the glistening delta land and the rolling wide heath of the tundra. While Chen was still earthbound he would squawk in an agony of frustration. But there came the day when he tried the injured wing, standing high on his strong legs, beating, beating the pinions against the chill wind of late August. Some snow had fallen the day before, and during the night a gale had swept from the polar cap across the Beaufort Sea. Ice glinted on the heath and sparkled from all the inlets and streams and bays of the delta.

The young gander could feel the chill of the wind on the scarred wing where the feathers had not fully returned. This new growing plumage showed in a whitish marking on the shoulder of his wing. But the only thing of importance on this day to Chen was the flying. The old goose's restlessness was with him too.

Soon he and thousands on thousands of his kind would sweep high, high across the black curve of the night sky before the giant hand of winter could close upon them. The long migration fraught with peril!

Was it the wheeling, the circling, the calling of other geese that told him? The excitement, the terrible urgency in the flock? Perhaps. He flapped his wings, thrusting them, beating them against the tides of air sweeping the tundra.

Honk, ho-o-onk, ho-o-onk. The excitement rolled up the long neck and burst from the wide gaping beak. Across the open ground he ran. Faster. Faster. His wings became a thunder in his own ears. Thrust with the legs! Kick with the wide feet! Ah, the wonder! The miracle!

The ground pulled away. The cold wind lifted beneath the great spread of wings. Up. Up. *Honk, ho-o-onk,* Chen's voice reached across the pale thin sky. Up! Sail high, high, high!

The other three young launched themselves into the air rising there just behind him; the old goose swept from above to fly before her small flock that now moved in a ragged kind of formation. As the old goose turned to fly there just ahead, Chen could feel the lift of air as it flowed over his mother's body. Ah, the flying was easier thus. And so he learned that lesson all wild geese know. It is this lesson that holds them in the V or the slanted line of flight. It is easier to fly in the wake of another. Thus in those high-flying V's it is only the leader who breasts the air alone, unaided. He cuts the flowing ocean of air as the prow of a ship cuts the sea. So tiring is this lead position that the responsibility is shared by a number of the strongest and wisest of the flock. When one tires another takes his place.

For the old goose and her young this day was spent in flying, in resting, in eating. The eating was of as great importance as the flying. The food was not so plentiful as in spring and early summer, and now it must serve a double purpose. As always there was the hunger of this day to be assuaged, but also it was necessary to eat enough to store the layer of fat beneath the skin and within the body for the long journey south to Tule Lake.

Until now the old one and her four had stayed separate, mingling not even with their own kind. Chen had scarcely been aware of the other geese that inhabited the delta islands and tundra. Now with the urge of flight a desire to come together also took hold of them. Small family flocks began to join one another as the ice islands of the Beaufort Sea had pushed together and clung. At first the flocks would meet and gabble and break apart, then regroup to part yet again. But by the end of August, Chen, his brother and his sisters were part of a gathering of geese that moved across the heath, along the shores, upon the river in a great noisy hoard that grew each day until there were over a thousand of them.

Mooshnuk, who knew that soon her family would fold the summer tents and start along the way back to Aklavik, came once more to climb a hummock and view the wide wild delta land. To look at the geese. Some of the migration excitement held even the girl today.

"Ah, Chen, where are you among those thousands, those hundreds of thousands of your brothers?" she murmured. She wore a heavy parka on this day, and the fur framed her round face, ruddy from the cold. Her bright dark eyes swept the wide land. "Soon you will leave. Those great wings will carry you far across the sky to a place where the sun shines each day and summer is not far away. But you will return, Chen."

From where she stood she was able to count a dozen of the huge flocks. Each flock stayed separate from the rest and seemed to respond only to its own sentinels, for occasionally all members of a group would fly into the air honking in alarm at some danger. They would wheel about, the sky dark with their wings, the air raucous with their voices. Mooshnuk knew that even beyond her vision there were other flocks and all were filled with the excitement of the coming migration.

Clouds had begun to sweep out of the northwest, streaming their cold gray banners across the pale sky. The wind had become steady and cutting. It was the tenth of September and Mooshnuk knew that all in this one day the summer had gone. The streamers of cloud melted into a dull overcast that advanced with each minute to swallow the rest of the sky. Already flakes of snow flew by on the rising winds. They did not settle to the ground, and when Mooshnuk turned to look into the northern sky they stung her face like icy splinters. When she glanced back at the landscape around her and at the geese marching across the heath, swimming the choppy waters of the Mackenzie, wheeling in the cold air, it seemed to her that the grayness of the clouds had spread to the land. All color was washed from the heath and the river and the birds; and the wind had swallowed all sound.

Tomorrow, perhaps tonight, the geese would fly. The great migration would begin. She turned away and trudged down the hummock, across the flats, bending forward against the rising force of the gale.

Chen's family flock had been with the great gathering of geese more than a week. Countless families made up the garrulous, restless mass. Usually there was an old goose and gander with several young, but there were also a certain number of single birds with three or four young like Chen's own mother. Occasionally there would be two parent birds with a single young one, sometimes with two or three. As in all years the hunters had claimed their toll. The mother wolf had feasted and given her warm milk to her pups. The snowy owl had eaten and carried food to its brood. The jaegers, the eagles, the glaucous gulls had taken eggs and young so they themselves could survive. And perhaps the wolverine had not returned to his forest home with empty belly.

Besides the hundreds of young that were of the same age as Chen, there were those of last season who as yet were unmated. The white-cheeks mate in their second year and these yearling birds would next spring have families of their own.

Though her gander was dead the old goose was content to be once more with the flock. For the first time since the eggs were hatched she could relax her vigilance a little. The sentinels of the flock kept watch for danger. It was good to have a few days of safety. The time of the perilous migration was near.

Chen became skillful at flying. Each day he spent much time rising into the air, wheeling about in short flights just above the gabbling flock. Occasionally when the sentinels would sound an alarm the hundreds of geese would take wing. The old gander's strength must indeed have been passed to his son, for soon Chen was rising with the skill and speed of the yearling geese. With the roar of thousands of beating pinions about him, he would spring aloft, the land would drop away and away, the horizon would expand until far below the flatness of the tundra would spread out to the very curve of Earth. And nothing was real to Chen but the beating of wings in the high sky.

Then would come the racketing cry of the old ganders. The long wild *h-o-o-onk* would pass through the ranks of the sailing geese. The sound would spread through the thin air and all creatures knew that winter was sweeping down from the north, that summer was ended.

The cold winds, the needling snow that had driven Mooshnuk from the hummock back to the family tents increased as the sun hung dim, burned-out just above the horizon. The gale brought a change in the flock. Chen saw the edgy nervousness of the old birds and of the yearlings and, as they did, he rustled his pinions, stretched his wings, gave his harsh cries. The old goose kept gabbling at Chen and her other three young ones, herding them together, as distraught as though some danger threatened. All of the parent birds in the great flock were similarly disturbed.

What danger was near? Some new peril! Chen thrust his neck high, pivoted his head this way and that, but around him was only a sea of gray-brown backs, a forest of stretching black necks and white cheek patches as the flock milled restlessly about.

The sun finally disappeared. The cold deepened in the gray twilight. The wind was a high steady whine across the bleak land. Suddenly then, with no warning, the flock took wing. All feet seemed to thrust at once as though the flock were one giant bird with one will. The beating of a myriad wings was around Chen, the whirring roar drowned even the ugly whine of the gale. In this moment his voice thrust up through his throat. His far echoing cry flew on the icy winds! As the flock circled, climbing ever higher, the honking cries increased until the northern sky was filled with the sound.

Mooshnuk, snug beneath her covering of robes, listened to the gale that shook the tent, listened to the winds sweeping the tundra, and as she listened, beyond and above the sounds of the storm, she heard the wild wonderful cries. The geese were truly flying this night!

"Goodbye, Chen," she whispered beneath the robes. "May nothing harm you through this long winter. Return in the spring, lovely Chen."

While the comfort, the warmth of her bed brought sleep to Mooshnuk, high in the night sky the geese circled again and yet again. The parent birds flew beside their young. Stragglers were urged to fall into line. After some time was thus spent in teaching the new ones the method of flight, some semblance of formation was achieved. The learning was rapid, for it became clear to the young ones that the flying was easier in the wake of another.

Now in a ragged V with one wise gander leading, the flock made a wide turning circle, then another. At last with steadily beating wings the lead gander wheeled toward the south. The flock swept in behind him. At last they were started on the long flight to Tule Lake. Two thousand miles they must fly to northern California.

The old birds in this flock had, years ago, made their first flight south with their parents. Each fall they returned to those same wintering grounds, taking each succeeding brood with them. Their parents before them had learned in this same way and the pattern had been started in the dim reaches of the past, perhaps in the time of the great ice ages. On this same night that Chen's flock had started its great flight to Tule Lake, there were other flocks aloft, fleeing the cold winter winds that pushed across the north pole behind them. Some would go to Tule Lake, some to wintering grounds in other parts of the United States or southern Canada. Some even as far as Mexico.

The great migration had begun. Hundreds of thousands of geese flew the sky that night. And danger flew beside them. Chen's wings beat steadily, steadily. From time to time he flung his voice upon the winds. To him the danger was nothing.

5   The Perilous Flight

Through the darkness of the night the flock moved southward. Never had Chen flown steadily in this way before. After a time weariness crept out along his wings. Beneath the white feathers of the scar the bone ached, but he kept the thrust of his pinions like a rhythm repeated a hundred times, a thousand times, ten times a thousand. Presently, miraculously, the weariness, the ache disappeared. There was only the wonderful flight with the excitement of the high sea of air and the wild cries that echoed back and forth from the spread arrowhead of the flock.

Others of the young on this first migration had neither the strength nor the spirit of Chen. For them this first night was an ordeal. The parent birds watched their own young carefully. When one of these fledglings seemed ready to fail an old one would fly close beside it and with soft urging gabbles cheer the faint spirit. After a bit with this help the youngster would find a second wind and the crisis would pass. Thus the first peril was surmounted — the peril of being left behind by the flock. This peril did not exist for Chen. With brave spirit he flew.

There was another danger. And it threatened all. Behind them out of the northern sky, sweeping from the eternal ice of the pole itself, raged the freezing gale. Had the flock delayed too long in leaving the nesting ground? In other years, other flights had been broken and scattered by the fierce early storms that seemed to come with no warning. If this storm tonight grew in strength and raced southward faster than the flying geese it could engulf them. Yes, death rode the gale behind them. The battering winds could scatter the flock, separating young from parent, gander from goose, brother from brother.

Men tell tales of finding the big geese, thus beaten from the sky, wandering dazed and forlorn. They can easily be taken by hand and neither do they take flight nor protect themselves. Death then seems almost a mercy. Ah, flee the storm, you wild ones, for life is better than death!

As the older geese pressed onward at a faster pace, Chen increased the thrust of his own wings. The urgency of the old wise ones was in some way carried to him, and his strength increased to meet the need. A few of the weakest were lost from the flock. Death in the freezing early storm would be their fate. But the mass of the flock escaped the hungry reaching fingers of the gale. Only the storm's forward winds brushed at their backs. And so, for most, the second peril was left behind.

The old goose flew safely with her four young ones. Did she remember the other years when her gander flew as leader?

The flock was weary. At last it drifted in a great ragged circle within the high bowl of the sky. The earth below still lay in the gray shadow of dawn. But the first golden rays of the sun touched the gliding birds, glinting from white throat patches, turning gray-brown bodies a warm copper hue. No longer did the wings beat in steady flight. Instead the geese let their outstretched pinions rest on the morning breeze as they circled lower, lower. During the hours of the night they had left the peril of the storm. They had flown almost due south while the storm that had swept from the north veered eastward so it no longer followed them. Other flocks were overtaken and many were destroyed. But Chen's flock had had luck with them.

Lower they circled, lower. The old birds warily eyed the open land, the lake below. The cold of the night had iced the water along the shore. At one end of the lake was a stand of trees and in places brush grew to the water's edge. Wisely the leaders shied from these covered areas. Instead they made for the open land that lay beyond the lake. The danger they now watched for was the danger that would threaten them each time they landed on the long flight.

Hunters from the edge of the arctic all along the miles of the flyways awaited the fall flight of the Canada geese. Even here on this first morning there could be danger, though they had covered a scant three hundred miles during the night and the land seemed wild and vacant. The flock spread out over the field. Busily, hungrily they ate, cropping the grass and small plants, shaking their tired wings, but all the time warily watching, watching. The lake and the fields were empty. But the brush — did something move there in the brush?

The cagey birds would not even approach the lake on this day but drank from a stream that forced its way between icy banks. Perhaps an hour was spent in resting, eating, drinking. Presently high in the sky came the voices of others of their kind. Another smaller flock flew a circle over the open land and the lake.

Down they came, weariness in every movement of their bodies, their wings. These had not been lucky; the edge of the storm had caught them and many of their number had been swept away by the terrible gale. The terror of that encounter had left its mark for now even the leaders seemed numbed, their wariness dulled. Down, down they drifted on outstretched wings. Chen could see them hovering just above the lake, above the reedy shore, above the brush.

Suddenly Chen's black eyes sharpened and in the same instant he gave a great honking cry. No other sentinel had been as quick to see the peril. Chen's voice sent his own flock rocketing into the air. Forgotten was the weariness. Too late the other flock across the lake took flight. In the stillness of the early morning a crashing boom rolled out of the treacherous brush. The poor storm-beaten birds scattered in wild confusion. But one fluttered to earth and did not rise again. The horror of the crashing sound came again and again and yet again. One more bird fell under the hunters' shots.

As Chen rose he looked down and across the lake. There stood two men, different in looks from the men of the Mackenzie delta land, but carrying sticks like those the others had carried, sticks that made crashing sounds. Chen's wounded shoulder ached in memory of that other time. Yet it was that painful memory that had sharpened his gaze there below, helped his quick eyes to see the hunter half rise in the brush. For it was Chen, not one of the brash yearlings nor yet one of the wise old ganders, who had given the warning on this first stop of the perilous flight. Yes, something of his father's spirit must have flown into Chen at the moment of his hatching.

Airborne, the flock headed south once more, rising in the sunny morn to ride the upper currents. For a time weariness again dragged at Chen, but as before strength came with the flying. He turned his head from side to side, his bright gaze sweeping the curved earth below. Away to the east wound the Mackenzie River, a golden ribbon in the early sun. The heath of the delta land began to give way to dark forests. Occasionally there would be a lake, once a chain of them joined by thin sandy strips of land, the small ones pale as the sky above, the larger ones dark blue in the center with the depth of the water, a light turquoise along the shallow shores.

On the far eastern horizon a line of darkness marked the sky, all that was left of the murderous gale. For the moment, at least, safety flew with the geese. But the stop at dawn had been broken by the hunters. As the sun rode higher in the sky both weariness and hunger forced the leaders to search for a place of safety where the flock could find food and water and rest. One so young as Chen would have no part in the choosing, yet he turned his head also, scanning the land that slipped past and behind as they pressed southward.

The weak and the young became exhausted and the formation straggled loosely across the sky. Three times a suitable landing place was found, but circling for a closer look proved each to have its own danger. One small lake had a grassy meadow along its western shore that might have been good for feeding, but brush crowded its eastern shore and some strange movement there sent the geese flying into the upper air once more with cries of alarm. Again they circled over an inviting spot only to turn south while still high in the air. A dog had barked somewhere below and some of the old geese knew of dogs and the danger that went with them. At the third lake, the flock had scarcely dipped downward before Chen's quick eyes saw a man standing on the sandy shore. This one made no effort to conceal himself but shading his eyes against the brightness of the sun gazed upward at the beautiful birds. Others saw the man and with gabbling and honking they swept on. No rest, no food for them in that spot.

Finally, when the flock had grown almost silent

with their weariness, the leaders saw to the west of
the line of flight that for which they had searched
— a great stretch of open water with marshy, reed-
filled flats along the shores, and beyond the reeds
fields of wild grasses, some of the stalks still heavy
with seed. Several times the geese swept over and
around this area. All seemed wild and safe, and even if
some danger appeared the miles of reedy shoreline
would hide them.

Down they came, down and into the center of open
water. For some time they were wary, looking this
way and that, gabbling nervously, scarcely eating or
drinking. But after a bit it became clear that at least
for the moment safety was with them. Then the
voices grew stronger and the geese swam this way and
that in the water, thrusting their heads beneath the
surface, tipping up to snatch the luscious water plants
from the silty bottom, for even here in the center the
great stretching pond was shallow.

The old goose and her four young ones swam together. Chen thrust at the water with his big webbed
feet and squawked at the pleasure of the wetness and
the coolness. He gobbled the water plants, thrusting
his head down and turning his tail skyward, snatching
the shallow-rooted greens into his bill and pulling with
great vigor. He sent showers of sparkling drops into
the air with his wings, then ran his head joyfully down
his back, stroking his feathers and pinions with his

beak, preening himself, until he was shining and lovely; then he went back to the eating again.

Ah, the water, the food, the resting of the weary wings! How good life was! Danger was forgotten. Only the sentinels remained wary and alert. But this was the time of resting and feeding, and fortune was with them for this spot was safer than most. For two days the geese lingered. Other flocks came to rest here also, but the marshy area was so large that even with thousands of birds it seemed a wild and empty place.

On the evening of the second day the air began to grow colder. The skim of ice thickened and even with no cloud in the sky winter seemed to lay its hold on water and land. With the coming of darkness they must fly again. The rest and the food had restored them and now the cold warned them to be on their way. Tule Lake was still far to the south, hundreds of perilous miles away.

The sky was black. A myriad of cold, bright stars sparked the night; no moon dimmed their brilliance. The air was still. The dark forests stretched below, but occasionally there was a speck of light as though a star had fallen and caught on some lonely spot. Perhaps a trapper, some hunter sat in the cold night beside a campfire. Or perhaps some brave heart who loved the solitude and only took from the wilderness for his own

needs. To these solitary ones, on this night, came the
voices of thousands of wild geese and they knew the
long northern winter had begun.

On through the night Chen flew. He could see those
geese nearest him in the darkness, could sense the hundreds beyond his sight, could hear the mighty rush
of a thousand wings. His own voice he added to the
high, wild sound of the migrating flocks. Even with
the feeding at the marshy lake his body was more lean
than it had been in the days of easy living at the delta.
But the leanness only added to his strength. Now his
wings became tireless, the pain of his old wound
nearly gone. He flew through the blackness of the
night, in the gray of dawn and in the bright gold of
the morning sun. When the flock grew weary there
was again the searching for a place to come to earth
in safety.

As the days passed, Chen became accustomed to
this pattern of life. The excitement of the high long
flights, the wariness and watching for danger on
landing. Some were lost to the hunters. Usually those
who died were the young who had not lived long
enough for wisdom, or the old who had lived beyond
their time and had now lost the strength and the
quickness to survive. There were a few in their prime
who also fell to the hunters' guns. Any goose or gander
who lost a mate in this way would fling its wild cries
of loneliness and anguish into the sky.

But always the flock continued on its southward flight and their dead ones and wounded ones were left along the path of the great flyway like the casualties of a moving army. Yet Chen survived and grew in strength and wisdom. Over a thousand miles they had flown. The stops had become short and now lasted only long enough for quick eating and drinking and partial resting of tired wings.

One morning with night paling to gray dawn the old ones began to keep a close watch on the land below. They had come this way before. Chen watched as the leaders watched. But for what did they search? The fat was gone from his body and hunger rode the sky. The bountiful life at the Mackenzie delta was far away. He scanned the land below with bright hungry eyes. Perhaps there would be a great marshy lake with the safety of reeds and a plentiful supply of water plants and seeding grasses along the shores! Hunger closed like a hand in Chen's body and he honked a hoarse protest.

But no marshy land appeared. Only the dark evergreen forests lay below. There were lakes, but they were small with sandy, rocky shores. There were no reeds for hiding, and the dangerous brush and trees crowded almost to the shorelines. On they flew. And yet the leaders watched closely. Would they never stop! What good to escape the hunters' guns and die of hunger in the high sky!

Chen's emptiness had become unbearable. He honked again and again in hunger and frustration. Finally though he heard the excited cries of the lead geese. Below still lay the evergreens, but when Chen looked far ahead he could see that the forest dropped away, though he could not see what lay beyond. Presently the whole flock swept over that edge of forest.

The evergreen highlands sloped gently away into the wide valley of the Peace River. Ah, the beautiful land, serene and golden with the stubble of harvested wheat stretching like fields of sunshine far, far on each side of the blue winding waters of the Peace River itself. These most northern and westerly lands of Canada's wheat belt lured the geese each fall, for in the stubble lay quantities of fat kernels left by the great harvesting machines. The sweet grain of no use to man would fatten the lean bodies of the migrating birds. And strength they would need, for even now before them rose the towering height of the Rocky Mountains. They must pass that forbidding barrier to reach the less harsh region of the Pacific flyway. Then the way would be easy to their home grounds and the safety of the Tule Lake Game Bird Refuge.

Three times the flock circled above the Peace River country. Chen, who had known only heath and forest, scanned the sunny fields below. There would be no sedgy water plants here! Down the old ones slanted though, leading the flock toward a pond with flat shores that lay at the edge of the wide golden valley land. Chen eyed the pond as they swept lower, lower. Would that small patch of water furnish food for this great flock? Where was the grass, where the heathy growth? Chen honked again in hoarse dismay.

The fields about the pond were wide and empty and safe. The old ones had scanned the land with care. Danger, great danger lay in this valley. Their wise eyes had seen the villages in the distance, had noted the scattered farmhouses. Men live in this place. Though scattered hunters in the lands they had already passed had taken a small toll from the flocks, now the great danger really began. Until they reached the safety of the Tule Lake Game Bird Refuge the deadly blast of shotguns would harry them. At each place they rested there would be some of this flock who would not take wing again.

With soft wary cackling the birds settled to earth. But Chen had forgotten all else except his great hunger. In one moment he discovered the fat fallen grain. Quickly he ate to fill the great emptiness within him. How sweet, how good were the wheat kernels! Strength was already returning to his tired and hungry body. The feathered army of geese spread over the land, gleaning the seeds as they went, and all the while the sentinels were wary, alert. These wise ones knew the danger here. Though the land was open with little place for a hunter to hide, there were the roads that wound through this farmland. Over these roads great huffing noisy monsters could roll and with these monsters came men with their guns.

Chen ate rapidly until the hunger was half quieted, then more slowly, gabbling to the old goose and to his sisters and brother. The family had remained together, never losing one another even in the hundreds of other birds. In the pleasure of eating Chen did not notice when the goose raised her head to look far across the grain field where the narrow black strip cut across the golden stubble. Others of the flock stopped to listen to the distant mutter. The sound grew to a noisy roar before Chen raised his head. Now his heart rocked him with sudden fear. Half the flock had ceased the gleaning and stood silently, heads high on a forest of stretching necks.

The young ones gabbled softly, nervously in alarm. Chen rustled his wings, ready for instant flight. Still the wise ones only stood and watched. Away across the fields on that strip of black Chen could now see the noisy monster. Its roar grew each second, but just as Chen was sure the flock must take wing, the terrible sound reached its height, then diminished until it was only a whisper, and the monster scooting along the black strip disappeared in the distance. Now the whole flock squawked and gabbled in nervous relief and went back to the eating. They drank and swam in the pond and rested in the quiet sun. Twice more there was the sound that grew and roared and flashed past and faded. The senseless fast-running beast looked neither this way nor that but only rushed along its narrow way. *Hauk-hauk!* Chen cried his scorn.

But presently one of the monsters came roaring down the black strip and stopped at a spot just opposite the flock. This time the roar quit with a suddenness, and the silence was then more fearful than the roar had been, for the beast did not go on its way. Three men climbed out and stood on the roadway watching the geese, then with their glinting sticks they came across the golden stubble.

Now the sentinels waited no longer. With loud cries of alarm they thrust the ground away. The entire flock rose as one bird and wheeled high, high, leaving the wonderful grain, the three hunters and the monster on its black strip far below. Even as he rose Chen watched those three with the deadly sticks. They grew small beneath his gaze as he mounted higher. Even so they were plain to see until suddenly they disappeared from sight. There had been no brush for hiding! Where had the three gone!

But the flock would not return to that spot so it mattered little. There were other fields. Miles on stretching miles of them. And other small ponds, and even where there were no ponds there were the streams

that slanted across the gentle watershed of the Peace
River. Yes, a land of plenty with grain and water for
the lean bodies, and sunny warmth for resting. Strength
would be needed. There was yet that Rocky Mountain
escarpment before them and the only way to Tule Lake
was over the jagged crest.

Rest and food they must have. These they could
get in the Peace River valley. But Chen was to learn
that here rest and food were dearly bought.

The flock flew over the golden valley until their
fears quieted. Once more they slanted down to a place
that looked empty and safe, a place distant from that
other where the monster and the three men had come.

The geese hovered for a moment over a pond, scanning the land. Yes, all was safe. In moments they
would be eating again, filling the emptiness that
had so quickly returned. Then there would be the
resting in the early sun. A thousand webbed feet
reached downward as the ground seemed to rise to
meet the geese.

And the peace of the land blew apart in a booming
crash! Chen pulled up his feet, flung himself upward
on flailing wings. Another crash and another. The
earth and sky burst with the thunder. Through the
crashing horror, Chen heard the ugly whistling spits
of sound about him. He shot straight upward, tilted
frantically away. The flock had broken apart. The ter-
rified birds whirled in all directions at once, but ever

upward until they were beyond the terrible sounds and the whistling pellets of death.

Chen tipped this way and that on wide wings and from the high safety watched the treacherous land below. How could it be! All had been safe about the pond and across the empty land. He could see the bodies of five fallen geese lying still, still in the morning sun. They had flown the long miles to perish thus in the Peace River valley. As Chen watched he honked a cry of dismay for the quiet golden land beside the pond now produced several men, each with a terrible stick. The men moved across to the geese that lay in the stubble.

Even in the terror of that sudden flight, the old goose and her young had stayed together. Now she gave a mournful, keening cry. Chen and his brother were safe, but only one sister remained. The old goose flew in several quick circles uttering her sad little cries. There were only three of her young ones left. First the gander had died on the northern heath; then one by one half of her brood had been taken from her. Would any reach the safety of Tule Lake?

Chen watched the hunters gather the fallen geese. From this height it was impossible to tell which was his sister.

Despite the danger and the loss of many to the hunters, the flock remained in the Peace River valley for several days. The lean bodies fattened a little, the tired wings rested and strength was gained for the high flight over the Rockies. The old wise ones remembered years when gales sweeping the towering summits had split the flock asunder beating some to the ground. And those died in the high snows. Others were thrust back into the Peace River valley where they endured the hunters until strength returned for another try at the heights. And always the danger that winter would close in before they could reach the safety of Tule Lake!

During this time of resting and eating Chen gained not only strength but also wisdom. He learned that the land could look safe to the eye but carry death for the unwary. Those hunters who had come in the monster had disappeared under Chen's gaze; the ones who had killed his sister had sprung from nowhere. And thus Chen learned that those men with the deadly sticks could conceal themselves. Only wisdom and a wary eye might discover the hiding places, for the hunters built blinds that from above blended with the surroundings and were almost invisible. Yet frequently the wise ones of the flock would discover the danger and with wild cries give the alarm in time for all to fly to safety, leaving the hunters disappointed, shivering in the early chill beneath the imperfect blind.

On the morning of the fourth day with the blackness of night still in the sky, the geese again were seized with the restless stirring. The air had become colder. The eating and the resting were at an end. Any moment now the flock would rise into the air as one great bird and the golden valley would be left behind. The urge of migration was with them. No regrets at leaving the sweet grain, no fear of the unknown dangers.

As the faintest gray touched the eastern sky the flock took wing. The land dropped away. The birds circled higher, higher; the air became cold, colder. The wide V of the flock climbed ever upward and Chen with the others sent his voice echoing against the massive peaks. Gone was the soft warmth of the valley. Now the air carried the freezing bitter scent of the great ice fields that hung the rocky ramparts. The arctic was hundreds of miles to the north, yet somehow now it had thrust its great hand up before the flock. How many could slip through the icy reaching fingers?

The birds became weary in the endless circling climb, and the spiral became more shallow. Now each wide turn gained them scarcely a hundred feet. Yet the peaks before them jutted high into the blast of wind that swept from the northwest. Chen honked hoarsely. Would this climbing last forever! But his strength was great and steadily he flew.

Already the very old and the weakest of the young were beginning to falter as the winds increased with each wide turn. How many would be torn from the flock on the jutting crest?

The stars in the eastern sky were paling with the light of dawn. The stars in the blackness of the western arch should still be hard and bright, yet they too began to disappear. Slowly, one by one they blinked out as though some ominous spirit crept between flock and heaven. By the time the birds had reached a height of six thousand feet the sun thrust a splinter of gold above the eastern curve of the earth.

Finally now it was plain to see what had blotted the stars from the western sky. Huge roiling clouds had boiled over the Rocky divide. Torn, pushed by the heavy winds, they reached above the peaks, a mighty breaking wave. The geese were specks of black in the immensity, tiny motes to be swallowed by the curving hollow of the storm. Their honking cries seemed lost on the wind.

Yet if they faltered now, winter might hold them in this hostile land. And Tule Lake was home. The clouds had taken all the peaks on the northern end of the granite spine. The leaders were headed for a low spot in the range where they would cross. Now it was hidden in the swirling mist. In clear weather, scarcely an hour's flight would have taken them through Pine Pass where the land rose to less than three thousand feet.

Now in the cold blast the leaders turned out of the

spiral and streaked rapidly toward the south along the face of the icy range. They raced the hurtling clouds that rolled before the winds swallowing peak after peak and filling the clefts and valleys between.

Twice the flock slanted in toward the mountains as though to attempt the crossing. Each time, the turbulent winds of the slopes and the swirling, sucking drafts of the canyons snatched at them and they tilted away again, fleeing ever southward, rising ever higher, until finally they were almost even with the tops of the most lofty summits. Even at this height the storm towered infinitely higher. One by one the peaks disappeared. Already Chen could feel the slicing icy splinters of sleet. Surely they must return to the wheat fields. And to the hunters.

As though the leaders thought of the hunters, they increased their wing beats. Chen saw the gap in the ridge even before the lead gander banked on a wing tip to streak westward. This would be their only chance. There would be no other way for them. The gap was shallow, only a little less high than the peaks around it. Some current of air had kept it clear, at least for the present. The storm itself had jumped the gap. The blackness of the clouds reached to left and right of the flock as they started the crossing. Even the slopes below the gap were wrapped in hanging streamers of mist. It was as though they were flying straight through a hole in the storm. Would the tunnel of clear air close before and behind, trapping them in the freezing gale?

On they flew. The turbulent winds beat at them from all directions. Headway was painfully slow. The weariness began along Chen's wings. This time the fatigue would not release him as before. With each passing moment it became more difficult to move forward. Without the steady force of beating wings, the wind would spit the birds out of the gap or hurl them against the jagged ramparts that now rose on either side. At first the rocky walls were far apart but as the flock proceeded the gap narrowed. The sucking drafts pulled them downward. The tops of the cliffy spires were lost in the clouds. Moment by moment the clouds lowered until the geese were flying in the dragging streamers of mist. The declivity became a canyon. Here the gale blew more mightily as would a river forced through a narrowing channel.

Twice Chen saw some bird, snatched by a terrible blast of air, whirl from the flock. Flailing wildly against the force each was swept still struggling out of sight. Once he himself was twisted about by a lash of wind. For one awful instant he was sucked away, downward toward the reaching craggy granite. Then the capricious current released him. With mighty, desperate thrusts he managed to regain his place behind the old goose.

Gradually though, the winds lost a little of their fury. Yet it had been this wind which had held the clouds aloft, for now the mists grew dense, the sleet fell more thickly, forming an icy crust on the wings of the brave birds. Still, on they toiled, the ice-heavy pinions dragging them lower in the canyon.

Chen honked against the weary struggle, but his voice was muffled by the pressing wall of cloud and sleet. Each thrust of his wings became unendurable. Was he to end this first long flight beaten down to perish in the snows of the pass!

How long, how long they flew between the perilous cliffs, against the smothering sleet! Then before Chen the old goose stretched her wings to rest easily on the air in a long slanting glide. Had she given up the struggle? Ah, the wicked end on the crags —

But then came the exultant cries of those who led the flock. And the cries were echoed down the long thin line of geese. Chen's own voice joined the racket even before he could see through the thinning mists. The descending flock cut down through the curtain of the storm. The blessed land slanted away below them, the diminishing ranges falling ever away toward the late sun that now hung visible, low in the western sky. The towering peaks of the Rockies lay behind them, still lost in the black storm.

The wild joyous cries of the flock filled the sky. At

last the weary pinions could rest on the long downward glide. Far, far to the west the Fraser River, snaking through its long valley, caught the gold of the afternoon sun. Now only the danger of hunters stood between the flock and Tule Lake.

6 Tule Lake

The boy sat in the boat looking at the wide flat country. To the north and the east the horizon was scarcely broken by the distant mountains. To the south lay the black hills of an ancient lava flow. And to the southwest Mount Shasta thrust its crown high into the morning air. The mountain was a solitary giant and on this particular morning a tremendous snow banner flew from the lofty summit.

Only the boy's eyes moved as he scanned the stretching shallow waters of Goose Lake. There were marshy bars of land that stood just above the water's surface and small islands with tules screening their shores. In the distance a raised delta supported an access road into the Refuge.

Goose Lake was part of the Tule Lake Game Bird Refuge, and Davey knew the access roads were for the use of the rangers and for anyone who wished to watch the tremendous gathering of wild wings that came slanting in across the northern skies each fall. Those who came desiring to watch or to photograph were welcome, but hunting was forbidden. Yet, Davey knew, there was still much sport for the hunters along the perimeter of the Refuge where the birds were not protected. But within the sanctuary the birds were safe, the fall migrants and also the resident birds that never flew the wide skies northward.

A man sat in the prow of the boat and he turned once to look at the boy. When the youngster pulled his gaze from the wild landscape and looked at the man, they both smiled a little but said nothing. It was clear no words were needed, for the exchanged glance was one of comradeship.

The boy's face was thin and pale. His clear bright blue eyes looked hungrily at the open country as though he had waited a very long time to see this place and now could not get enough of it. He hunched into the heavy wool jacket. It was too large for his slight frame. He pulled the hood partly over the thick straight thatch of his blond hair, thrust his hands into the sleeves. Then he settled again to the silent watching.

Snow had fallen during the night, making a thin icy crust on the brown mottlings of land, on the bars and flat islands. Now the October sun as it stood higher in the sky began to melt this skim. Yet the gusty breeze remained chill, skirling across the open water, making wind shadows on the flat surface.

After a bit the man said, "Guess we'd better go back now, Davey. No use to overdo on the first day, eh?"

"Not so soon, Sam." The blue eyes were pleading. "I'm not really cold yet, honest. It's even better than your letters said. Why, it's even better than I used to imagine. Look, Sam! There in the shallows near the reeds, a great blue heron! He stands so still. And the tern just above, look at him soar! Oh, Sam, it's so good to be finally here!"

The man smiled, his gray eyes squinting a little in the bright, translucent autumn light, but he shifted the oars and said softly, "There's tomorrow, Davey, and the next day, and all the rest—"

Then above the sounds of the birds that seemed all around them, above the sound of the breeze and the lapping water, came the wild high honking of geese. The boy shivered a little as he heard the distant voices and his whisper was breathless with excitement.

"Geese! Let's just see them come in, Sam, then we'll go."

The man had stopped working with the oars. The two sat motionless in the gently rocking boat, watching to the north, listening to the faint gabbling that grew louder with each passing moment. Now they could see the advancing V, and the man pushing with the oars concealed the boat in the reeds. As the flock drew nearer the black specks became individual geese.

"Canadas," Sam breathed, but neither he nor David moved.

The boy could feel his heart thump against his ribs. The long dreary days in the hospital were not even a memory for this moment. As the great birds drew closer, closer, the boy thought surely his own excitement would not let him remain still. "The wise birds," Sam had called them. Would they be too wise to land near the boat?

On came the flock, lower, lower, until each bird was visible. The mighty curving wings, which would not yet be content with only the gliding, thrust with slow, majestic rhythm.

"Not too low, not too low," Davey sent the silent warning. There would be the hunters out on the firing line, along the perimeter of the Refuge. Even as the boy had feared there came the distant boom, boom of shotguns. Novice hunters. The wise geese had come in high enough to escape the deadly pellets. Now on they sailed over the safe waters, the beautiful gray-brown bodies, lean from the terrible journey, the weary wings beating, gliding, tilting from side to side as the birds warily watched the wind-riffled water, the islands and bars and reedy shores.

Ah, the perilous flight was finally ending. Tule Lake Refuge! Safe winter home! Safe from the hunters. Safe from the freezing black night of the arctic. Safe from hunger, for within the sanctuary itself there were grain fields planted especially for the birds. And even outside the Refuge was the wild spreading country where the geese could forage for seeds and grasses. But there care must be taken, for safety ended for the birds in the unprotected lands.

The geese sailed over the man and the boy. Davey moved only his eyes to watch. The wonder of the great bodies and tremendous wings! So close! The glistening white throat markings, even the black alert eyes were plain to see. But on across the reeds, across the water and over a narrow neck of land the flock skimmed without alighting.

The cries of the migrants, the muffled whoosh of their wings stirred a family of mallards bobbing on the water, excited a colony of grebes who disappeared beneath the surface of the lake with a flick of

upturned stubby tails. The blue heron remained motionless, intent on his solitary fishing, nor did the man
and the boy move.

Davey thought he must be content with the one pass
above the boat. Perhaps the geese had seen them. He
watched the flock as it dropped lower there beyond
the bar. Already the first birds were reaching downward with stretching legs when something startled
them. Weary though they were, the hundreds of
birds thrust back into the air to wheel once more with
loud cries. Over they came again, turning in a great
circle to sweep back above the boat. Davey could
scarcely breathe with the excitement. Ah, maybe,
maybe — Yes, they were settling! And wonderfully
close! The flock swept in, down, reached legs and feet,
alighted with grace and precision. They were near
enough for Davey to see the soft pattern of their
feathers, the dense creamy down of their breasts and
the ever alert, wise eyes. The gabbling and clattering was wondrously noisy. The boy's intense eyes were
round with excitement.

At first it seemed the flock was a single milling mass
of geese. Yet as Davey watched he saw that even
within the flock small groups stayed together and he
remembered that Sam had told him how each family
was loyal to its own members. A great number of these
family units were clearly a goose and gander and several young, but Davey's heart was touched by the soli-

tary birds who swam a little apart from the rest with a dejected air of loneliness. These would be the ones who had lost mates, perhaps this season, perhaps another year. For Sam had said some geese and some ganders did not remate again or at least stayed single for several seasons, grieving for the lost mate. Ah, the poor lonely ones.

As the geese became assured that this was a place of safety, the family groups separated a little more widely from the mass, swimming here and there in the blessed haven, seeming to rejoice that the long flight was at an end. Several such groups gradually drew closer to the concealed boat. There was an old one who must have lost its mate this season, for only three young swam with the old bird, and no other adult joined them.

Still how could that one be too sad with three such beautiful young! Davey wondered about the long flight they had made and what had happened to the lost mate and the others of this family. Had the hunters killed them? Ah yes, yes, there had probably been hunters, for look at the mark along the shoulder of the largest young one.

Davey scarcely moved his lips and his voice was only a breath. "Sam, see that one has been wounded, see where the feathers are white across its shoulder."

"You're probably right." Sam spoke no louder than had the boy.

Even that slight sound set the geese to churring nervously and they immediately moved off in the opposite direction, each leaving an arrowhead wake of spreading ripples in the greenish water.

The man turned to the boy now and the movement sent the nearest birds into the air in quick alarm, but a recollection of the safety of the place was with them and most of the flock only swam away toward the far shore and those that had taken wing settled once more.

"Well, we saw them, Davey." Sam smiled. The skin of his face was like tanned leather from long exposure, and the creases of his cheeks and the lines about his eyes settled easily into the smile.

The boy gave a blissful nod. But he shivered as a gust of chill wind bent the reeds. The man, seeing this, pulled at the oars, sending the boat out across the water toward the raised delta where the road lay.

The geese gave their hoarse scolding cries, but few took wing and most only swam farther along the lake, stretching their necks and eying the boat with the man and boy who carried no deadly sticks. Davey watched the flock even after he reached the raised land. He could still see the one with the white shoulder patch. That one, because of the mark, seemed different and a single bird that he might remember. Perhaps he might even see it again during the long winter. There was a sudden surge of happiness within the boy when he thought of spending the weeks here with his uncle.

"Let's get the boat on the truck, Davey," the man called. "Those birds will be here all winter. Right now let's get back to the house and have some hot soup to chase the chill."

"Okay," the boy answered quickly, smiling at the man. But he was shivering all over from the cold. "Do you think we'll see that flock again?"

"Or one just like it." The man hauled the light aluminum boat up the steep bank and with the boy's help swung it into the back of the dark green truck.

"There isn't a flock *just* like that one," Davey said puffing a little and the man turned to watch him closely, the shadow of a frown creasing between the heavy brows.

"I'd like to see the big young one with the white on its wing again," the boy continued.

"Don't set your heart on *that*." The man laughed his soft laugh and the kind gray eyes, worried, looked down into the big intense ones of the boy. "There are thousands and thousands of Canadas here during the winter. Not much chance you'll see that same bird."

Davey climbed into the high truck. The door made a tinny crash in the silence of the long empty delta road. The man climbed in on the other side.

The boy said nothing until the truck was rolling. "But I might."

"Might what?" the man asked not taking his eyes from the roadway.

"Might see the one with the wound mark on its shoulder."

There was a silence between them as the man shifted gears. After a bit he said, "Well, you just possibly might."

And the green truck, with the words "U.S. Forest Service" on the door, jounced along the graveled delta road.

Not many had been lost to the hunters on the last part of the flight. Now the flock rested safely within the Refuge. Chen swam with the old goose and his brother and sister. What comfort to fold the weary wings!

The nervous urge of migration was stilled. Here was the safe home of winter. Now he filled himself with the succulent water plants. When the flock tired of the water and the wariness had quieted, they moved out across the stretching fields.

To Chen the winds did not feel chill and the October sun filled him with contentment and warmth. Slowly the great hunger was satisfied. On the land there were the fields with grasses and grain. The sweet kernels began to fatten his lean body. As the days passed he saw more people than he had ever seen in the far north. The flock kept a distance from any men who appeared and scolded loudly at those who invaded this domain. But the birds were wise and there was little fear in the scolding for the men who came here carried no deadly sticks and did not molest the creatures of the Refuge.

One day Chen was eating hungrily at the grasses a little distance from the rest of the flock. Busy with the food he moved close to a stand of woody brush. Presently some instinct made him raise his head to stare uneasily about. The sun made the black of his head and neck shine and the white cheek patches glisten; the warm buff of his back and the thick down of his breast looked wondrously soft. The pale feathers of the scar were plain to see.

"Oh, you are a beautiful bird! I knew I would see you again."

The voice was only a breath in the chill breeze, but there was no movement to startle Chen. David sat very still there at the edge of the brush. The thinness of his face had begun to fill out and his cheeks, so pale on that first day, were touched with color. He watched now as Chen moved warily toward him. The boy could see the big webbed feet step hesitantly, carefully through the tufty grasses, and as he watched, the sun glinted on something fastened about one of the young gander's legs.

"You aren't as wild as the others." David spoke softly. Again Chen hesitated, his black, bold eyes watching that one who sat quietly and spoke to him. That young one of the Mackenzie River delta had talked thus, and she had been kind. So slowly the bird drew closer, lisping, churring nervously, fascinated by the motionless boy who carried no deadly stick and whose voice was quiet like that other friend.

"What a bold bird you are," continued the boy. His voice shook a little from the excitement and from the cold November wind. "What is that around your leg? Were you caught once? That's no accident; I can see it's been carefully fastened."

Now Chen had come as close as he dared. He stood higher than the seated boy. Moving his head quickly, nervously from side to side he gazed at the motionless one, listened to the soft voice. With his curiosity unsatisfied, caution finally forced him to move away. Several times as he retreated he stopped to gaze back at the boy who still sat unmoving.

Not until Chen had rejoined the flock, losing himself among the other birds, did David rise to his feet. He moved stiffly for a step or two. The long sitting in the cold had numbed him, but after a dozen yards he moved easily across the rough ground until he came to the road. There he turned about and gazed back at the geese. He could hear their gabbling as they ate happily, safely in the grain. All of him felt alive as he finally turned and moved off down the road. He could feel his heart beating steadily, strongly within him.

This was the first of all of his fourteen years that that same heart had not held him a pale and breathless invalid. The only thing that had made the days alive for him then had been Sam's letters, the letters that glowed with the sunshine and the freshness of the wide country. That were filled with the birds and wild things of the Refuge.

And now I'm here! David's thoughts were jubilant.

He remembered his fear of the operation, but the terrible day had come and strangely the fear had quieted. And the day itself in no way lived up to his previous dread. All had gone well and there had remained only the discomfort of recovery. The surgeon had made the ailing heart as sound as though it had never given trouble at all.

And then there had been the letter from Sam!

— come and spend the winter with me. Your mother and father could use a trip after the worry and I'm lonely here since Madge has gone —

Madge had been Sam's wife and David remembered the long stretch two years ago when Sam's letters had stopped for months when she had died.

— the school is good in town and there's a bus for the kids who live here at the Forest Service station.

*Tell your mother to be kind to her old brother, and
to let you come up and keep me company, Davey. It
would be good for you and good for me —*

And David could hardly wait for his mother and father to come to the hospital that evening. There had
been hesitation because worry had become a habit
with them, but when Dr. Bentley had said the idea
was a good one, everything had worked out right.

Now David could see the green truck away off
down the road, small and solitary in the flat landscape.
As he drew near, he could see Sam's tall, rangy form
and the man gave an easy wave before turning to
some task about the truck.

"I saw 'im again," Davey said as he climbed onto
the high seat. The man thrust the key into the igni-
tion, started the motor.

"Saw who?" he said after the truck was under
way.

"That goose with the scarred shoulder."

"Well, that's luck for you." The man reached a big
hand and gave the boy's shoulder a little shake. "He's
probably a gander, very large for a young bird. It really
was luck, you know, to see him again out of all the
thousands."

"He came right up to me."

The man glanced at the boy, interest in his face.

"They're usually pretty cagey. How did you man-
age it, Davey?"

The boy twisted in the seat to face his uncle. "I saw the geese from way down the road and I crawled through the brush and sat real still just at the edge of the field. The one with the scar seems less scary than the others. Or maybe he just has more curiosity. Anyway I'm not the first person he's been close to."

"How's that?"

"He's got a piece of metal fastened around one leg."

"Oh?" The man stopped talking for a moment while he pulled the truck out onto the main highway, pausing for a fast-moving car that went whizzing down the asphalt strip. "He must have been banded. It would be interesting to have a closer look at that band, then we'd know where he came from."

"Oh, Sam, do you suppose — could we catch him, do you think?"

"If we could find him again, maybe we could. I'll show you some bands when we get back to the house and you can see if they're like the one fastened to the gander's leg."

Sam's house was one of a dozen tucked in the lee of a low ridge and surrounded by grass that now was beginning to brown with the autumn frosts. David loved the big kitchen with its sunny yellow walls, reddish brown floor. Even on a gray day it was cheerful and bright and warm. Here Sam cooked the hearty stews and soups, sometimes a steak, the crusty home-made bread, all the good food that was filling out the boy's frame.

Today after they had shucked jackets and sweaters, Sam brought a wooden box from his own room and set it on the big kitchen table. He rummaged for a moment in the contents.

"Here," he finally said, handing a narrow flat strip of metal to his nephew. "Did it look like this?"

"Nope," said the boy after a quick inspection. "It was heavier, more silvery looking."

The man frowned a little. "He didn't act tame enough to be somebody's pet?"

"No-o. At least I don't think so. He did come awfully close though. But he was smart. He stayed far enough away so there wasn't a chance of my catching him."

Sam rubbed a hand through his dark grizzled hair and the frown remained on his face. "I hate to see that kind of banding. Too tight and a bird can lose a foot, too loose it'll maybe catch on something and the bird can't get away. Then it'll starve to death or fall prey to a fox, a wolf, sometimes up north a wolverine."

"Well, whoever put this one on knew how to do it," David assured the man. "There wasn't anything wrong with the gander's foot and the band seemed snug enough not to catch on anything."

Sam put a big frying pan on the stove and splashed a dollop of golden cooking oil in the bottom. In a few minutes the good smell of frying onion filled the kitchen.

Davey came to stand beside the man. They enjoyed each other's company, sometimes with few words between them. Now the silence held until they sat down to eat the browned beef and onions. There was a crisp green salad and thick slices of the home-made bread and butter.

"I'll tell you, Davey. I won't have time for maybe a week to help you try to catch that young gander. Pack yourself a lunch tomorrow though and I'll drop you off at the place you found him today. Maybe if you watch you can tell if we'd be likely to find him there again." Sam had finished eating and now he tilted back in the straight chair, stretched. When he settled down, his kind eyes searched the boy's face. "You're feeling okay these days?"

"I feel so darned *good*, Sam. Why, I guess from being about the most sickly kid there ever was, I'm the most healthy!" The boy's laugh was pure pleasure.

The man stood up and placed an affectionate hand on his nephew's head. "Well, time to turn in, Davey, if you're going to get the jump on that young Canada of yours."

"Okay." Davey got up and started for the door and then he turned back to look at the man. His face had become serious. "I don't want to catch him and

keep him, Sam. It would be terrible to have those wonderful wings and be shut up where you couldn't fly."

Sam nodded and smiled his slow smile. "I know."

And there was the understanding between them
with no further words.

7   The Trap

The next dawn was gray and cold with silent flakes drifting out of the overcast. Davey dressed quickly and hurried down to the kitchen. Here it was already warm and smelling of bacon and coffee. Sam was sitting at the table, a thick mug of the rich black brew before him.

"A few head of cattle from one of the ranches got away last night and they're down in one of the Refuge grain fields. I'll have to go and help get them out. You still want to look for that young gander, Davey?"

"I sure do," the boy said eagerly.

"Eat your breakfast then, and put on a sweater and your heavy parka and mittens. It feels like winter outside."

Less than an hour later the man had dropped the boy off at the field where Chen had been. It was only a couple of miles back to the house so it was decided that Davey would be on his own and return to the station when it pleased him. He waited for the truck to disappear in the distance, then made his way across the field now wet with the instant melting of the big softly drifting flakes.

Today the field was empty of geese. A small hawk hovered on rapid wings; a few gulls searched among the grasses, flying up with nervous, raucous cries from time to time. There were terns wheeling and darting through the gray air after invisible insects. Grebes, mallards, redheads, a few loons stirred the waters of the lake and made the air noisy with their voices. The solitary blue heron again kept his motionless vigil. But there were no geese in this field.

For a while Davey sat quietly at the edge of the brush. It was here he had seen the scarred gander. He hoped the same luck would be with him today. Across the waters of the lake from the distant curve of shore a flock of geese came swimming. He could hear the high gabble of their voices, but as they drew near they seemed not as large as the birds of the young gander's flock and when finally they marched ashore Davey thought them probably cackling geese, marked as the Canadas but smaller and without the regal bearing.

He watched them for a while but the ground was wet and cold, so finally he stood up and stretched the stiffness from his legs. The cackling geese, scolding sharply, moved back into the water and swam some distance from shore.

To drive the chill from his body Davey climbed to the raised roadway, strode rapidly along, liking the feel of the gravelly surface beneath his feet and the cold kiss of the flakes upon his face. His eyes were eager to see everything in the wide flat land. Presently he came to the highway, stretching empty in either direction. It marked the boundary of the Refuge. For a moment the boy hesitated. Well, the day was his own and there was no reason to stay within the Refuge. He felt a little thrill at the prospect of exploring the new country. In moments he was across the asphalt strip, had scrambled down the bank to the flat of a marshy field. It was muddy and sedgy here, but presently the ground rose in gentle hillocks and the footing became firm, and in a few hundred yards Davey found himself along the reedy shores of a lake.

There was the distant sound of a car and when he looked back he was surprised to see how far behind he had left the highway. The car, like a toy on a conveyer belt, moved steadily along and disappeared, leaving the land empty again.

He had no way to tell the time but when he became hungry he guessed that it must be the middle of the day. The endless sky was still leaden and the flakes continued to sift down, too wet to last upon the ground. But surely it was noon. Hunger rumbled in his stomach and Davey found a spot half sheltered from the wet beneath a low arching bush. He opened the lunch that Sam had packed for him and eagerly bit into the meat sandwich with the hearty, crusty bread.

All the while his watchful eyes scanned the water, the fields. Even here outside the Refuge the wild life was plentiful. By thus sitting quietly, Davey found that the birds and small animals forgot that a stranger was there beneath the bush and they moved about freely before him. There were the busy rodents of the fields; and along the water's edge a muskrat swam, the arrowhead of ripples revealing him even though he moved as silent as a shadow. There were countless birds. Twice flights of geese swept low above the water so that Davey could hear their wings and see their markings. Was the young gander in either of those flocks?

Sam had been right. The chance of seeing that one Canada was slight indeed. In the distance several times there was the dull boom of shotguns. Would those hunters find the young gander?

He had finished eating but still sat motionless in the gray, quiet cold. When finally he had grown too chilled to stay thus longer and thought of moving on, he was held by the sound of geese honking across the sky. Presently in sailed the flock, down they settled. How lightly they came to earth!

The flock spread over the field, busily eating, churring and lisping and making their usual racket. Davey's interest sharpened and he watched closely. This flock was about the size of the one with which the gander flew. Could he possibly be here? It seemed hopeless to look for him in the great mass of milling birds.

Chen had rested from the long migration flight. His lean body was rounding again with the good grain and grasses of the Refuge, with the aquatic plants of Goose Lake and Tule Lake. The first week or two the flock stayed well within the sanctuary, eating, resting, gabbling happily. Chen and his brother and sister and the old goose were safe, contented. Usually they stayed together within the flock. Occasionally though Chen's boldness and curiosity made him eager to look at this new world on his own. Then he would skirt the far edges of the flock searching the reeds, the low sparse brush, the fields. Thus he satisfied both appetite and curiosity. And there had been much for both to feed upon!

There had been the day that beside a strip of brush he had come upon a man-child, a motionless one who carried no deadly stick. Chen's heart had beat quickly with fright but he had drawn close to look at that one who somehow reminded him of the friend who had poulticed his wing far away beside the Mackenzie. But caution had finally turned him back to rejoin the flock and the nervously calling goose.

The safety of the Refuge lulled the geese; the old dangers became dim, almost forgotten. After a time they sailed even beyond the boundaries of the Refuge. At first their luck was good with the distant sound of guns the only reminder that safety was never a sure thing. Chen loved the easy flying and the plentiful food and the exploring of the new lands. He forgot the dangers entirely. And because of that his freedom was nearly taken from him.

It was a gray still morning with wet soft flakes drifting out of the overcast. The flock grazed during the early dawn and swam the waters of Tule Lake, feeding along the reedy shores in the shallow green waters. But their wings became restless so presently some rose lazily into the air. With none of the discipline of migration, the others straggled after. They made a slow circle above the lake, the second turn taking them beyond the highway, beyond the edge of the Refuge. Caution half forgotten, they slanted down toward a field where the grasses seemed thick and inviting. For a moment after landing the wariness returned and they looked nervously about, clattering and gabbling to assure themselves they had not been foolish in landing. And truly all seemed safe so they fell to eating.

The old goose and her three were near the outer edge of the flock and Chen, still a prodigious eater because of his great size, moved farther and farther afield. How good the eating was, far better than within the Refuge! He had found a pile of sweet grain as big as his own head! Quickly he gobbled it down. And beyond, the golden kernels were scattered thickly. He moved along pecking with great industry, unaware of the sound of one of the noisy monsters on its distant strip, unaware that the monster stopped and a man climbed out to stand beside the highway and look across the fields at the geese. A few of the sentinels of the flock eyed the man warily but not until he scrambled down the roadside bank did they begin to uneasily gabble, stretching their long necks to watch his progress.

But Chen was lost in the joy of the plentiful grain that was leading him into the edge of the brush. He did not see the boy who sat perfectly still in the low growth. The boy's eyes were shining with excitement for the pale blaze of feathers across the young gander's shoulder was plain to see, and once when Chen stepped high the dull gleam of metal about his leg showed for a moment.

The trail of grain continued a few feet beyond the edge of brush and the gander made quick work of scooping it up with eager beak. Then suddenly he stopped. There was a strange thing before him. It was not brush nor reed nor rock and with curiosity he eyed it. Strange indeed, with a lacework of wire through which Chen could easily see. Within lay a pile of the good grain. Warily he inspected this thing that enclosed the grain. He pecked at the metal once or twice. The front was entirely open so all he need do to reach the food was to step through and it was his.

Dimly he was aware of the nervous cries of the flock and among their voices he could hear that of the old goose calling to him. If he was going to eat the grain he must do so quickly. The flock might take wing at any moment.

Now with no hesitation he stepped inside that odd enclosure. Quickly, the grain! He thrust his beak into the kernels. Gulped their goodness. Thrust again.

Crash!

His heart gave a great surge of fear. At last the grain

did not matter. He tried to turn around. He could not. Terror gripped him. He tried to back out of the open side where he had entered. Panic seized him. He could not back through the opening! It had disappeared. The trap was as solid behind as to either side and before him. He flailed his great wings until down and feathers were left clinging to the wires. *Hauk-hauk!* He called his frustration and terror to the silent gray sky.

When he stopped his effort for a moment he could hear the cries of the sentinels. Then he honked in dismay for the beating of many wings came to him and the shadow of the departing flock presently swept over the cage. Once before in his life he had been alone, that time when the hunters of the Mackenzie delta had wounded him. But then he had been able to scurry through the tundra growth and escape. Now he was trapped. For trap it was, set for just such a young unwary one as Chen. Oh, foolish greedy hunger! Was this the end of his free flying of the wide skies?

Again he sent his cry upon the air. He beat his wings until he was bruised, exhausted. But even then he would not have stopped but a shadow fell across the cage and a soft voice spoke.

"Who could have set this cruel trap?" David said. "Poor thing. Don't be so frightened. If I can I'll let you out. Be still, be still. I think someone stopped on the highway. That's why your flock flew away."

David had never thought to be so close to the young gander. Now as he worked at the trap he looked at the beautiful glossy feathers of Chen's back and wings and the thick fluff of down where it puffed at the forward edge of the wings. The gander tried to turn his head in the narrow space and his beak rattled against the wires. So fascinated was the boy that he stopped his efforts with the cage to inspect the bird more closely.

"Maybe I can see what's on that leg band!" David was excited by the sudden thought and bent quickly to look.

The movement startled Chen and he flailed wildly for a moment. David spoke softly and moved no further until the gander quieted. Now carefully he put his face close to the ground, peering through the heavy wire mesh. The metal anklet was plain to see.

"Yes, there *are* words," David breathed. "I can't quite see all the letters though."

With great care not to frighten the trapped creature the boy edged about the cage waiting when necessary for the gander to move and bring a new angle of the band to view. When he had almost completely circled the trap David was suddenly aware that there was someone, something else in the brush. There were the sounds of breaking twigs and through the ground came the vibration of careless walking.

Quickly, silently the boy began working at the fastening of the trap. He could see that the door had dropped into place, sliding down grooves on either side of the opening. In sliding it must have jammed, for now he tugged at it with all his strength and could not budge it. Closer came the footfalls. David could see the nervous tremor of the gander's wings. But the foolishness had left Chen. Now he was wary and wise and silent. It was almost as if he knew the boy meant him no harm but that the other thing crashing through the brush was an enemy.

Frantically David tugged. He felt as if his own freedom was held within the trap. Closer came that one in the brush. It would be the man who had set this trap. Otherwise he would not come so straight, so unerringly. David glanced anxiously about. He was not sure that what he was doing was right. Perhaps he was robbing a legal trap! In the moment of that thought he saw the figure of the man, plunging along through the low growth.

No caution now! David stood up, yanked with all of his strength at the trap door. With a sudden screech of metal it flew up, and at the same instant the man bellowed.

"Hey you, boy, what're you doing! Get outa there!"

Chen could not see that freedom was behind him. The man's shout made him freeze as the wild will do.

With no thought of the gander's beak, David reached into the cage and catching the bird's legs yanked him out through the opening. In an instant Chen saw that freedom was his.

With a loud cry and the mighty thrust of feet and legs he sprang into the air. David could feel the wind from the beating pinions. Almost into the man's face the gander flew. Then he hurled himself aloft, his cry racketing through the cold gray world.

All had happened so rapidly that the frightened flock was still aloft, circling above the lakes and fields. In moments Chen had joined them, answering the old goose's cries with relieved honking and gabbling.

But David was left to face the angry man.

"Just why did you do that! I'm tryin' to catch me a goose. You dumb kid. Who's your pa? You got no right to meddle with somebody else's stuff!" The man, face red with anger, towered above the boy.

David tried to keep his voice steady. "I'm staying with my uncle. His name's Sam Douglas. He's a ranger at the Refuge."

"Oh, one of *them*." The man laughed a short laugh. It wasn't a nice laugh and David saw that the other no longer glared at him but instead the dark little eyes shifted away to the trap and the door which now lay on the ground. "No use to talk to *him*. Them rangers won't even let a man shoot for his dinner no more, 'thout tellin' him he's crossin' some thought-up line where the game can run acrost and say 'Kings-x' like a kid playin' hide 'n' seek. My pa and his pa before him lived in these parts when there wasn't no silly rules and a man could do as he liked. Now it's don't shoot this and don't shoot that and even what you can shoot just shoot for a few weeks when we tell you it's okay!" He snorted with anger and frustration.

"There wouldn't be anything for anybody to shoot at all," said David, "if everybody still shot the way your grandpa and pa did. There probably wouldn't even be very many birds to *see* to say nothing of shooting."

"I wasn't going to kill that one in the trap anyways," the man said, some of the anger beginning to leave his voice, and once he glanced uneasily over his shoulder. "I was going to clip her wings and keep her for laying eggs. I'd a caught me a gander too."

"That one was a gander, I think," David said, his clear blue eyes looking directly into the stranger's face. He had seen the uneasiness of the other when he had looked back toward the highway.

The man gave his short mirthless laugh again. "A lot a dumb kid like you'd know about it. Anyways I'll just take my trap along and set it where you can't meddle with it. After this just stay outa my way or I'll tan you, no matter who your uncle is."

So saying, the man yanked up the wire cage and without another word crashed off through the brush.

The snow was falling more thickly and the cold had deepened. By the time David reached the house, the gray day had turned to a gloomy dusk. The windows glowed orange in the early darkness. He caught a movement of the curtains as he climbed the front steps and knew Sam had been watching for him. The good warm cooking smells swept out with the opening of the door. A surge of affection filled the boy when he saw the man's rough, kindly face full of concern. David knew he was late but all the man said was, "Have a good day, Davey boy?"

"I'm sorry I stayed out so long, Sam. I guess I just lost track of the time."

"That's easy to do. I drove past where I dropped you and didn't see you around. I thought probably you'd tramped off looking for that gander. Any luck?"

"Wait'll I tell you —" The boy's face was eager, his cheeks flushed from the warmth of the room after the November cold.

"Come on in the kitchen and tell me about it while I dish dinner. Chili beans with lots of meat —" The man winked at the boy knowing it was one of his favorites.

David told about the whole day, about leaving the Refuge and watching the wild things from his place in the brush. About the gander and about the trap and the man who had been so angry over the loss of what his trap had caught.

Sam laughed as he slid the steaming bowl of chili before his nephew. "Don't let that man's temper bother you. Sounds like Brennan Dover. He thinks the whole territory belongs to him because his grandfather fought Captain Jack and the Modocs. His father owned one of the first ranches around here. But it's illegal to set traps like that and Brennan knows it. You did just right. So you saved the gander! You're sure it was *the* gander?"

"I'm sure. And Sam, I got to read his leg band." David's eyes were bright with the memory of the beautiful bird. Then he laughed ruefully. "Not that it did any good. I don't know what the words meant. The first one was in big letters. 'Chen.' And then below in smaller letters, 'Aklavik.' "

"I've heard of the last one, Aklavik. That's a small town in northern Canada near the Mackenzie River delta, above the Arctic Circle. The delta is one of the main breeding grounds for Canada geese. I know that some of the geese here come from the Mackenzie delta."

"Would Chen be a place or someone's name?"

"I don't think it's a place. It could be a person's name. Somehow it sounds more like a name for the gander, though."

"Chen," the boy mused. "It would be a good name for him. When he sort of chatters like he's nervous it does sound a little like *chen-chen-chen*."

They were silent for a bit as they ate. Then suddenly David sat straight in his chair.

"Why can't I write to Aklavik! Since it's a little town maybe everyone would hear of the letter and whoever banded the gander — whoever banded Chen — might answer!"

"If you can get an answer you'll know why that gander is so tame and how he happens to be banded. Maybe even about the scar on his shoulder." The man sounded as excited as the boy.

"But who can I send the letter to in Aklavik? Who would be willing to show it around to everybody?"

"The Hudson's Bay Company post," Sam said, and at David's questioning look continued, "There's a post store in a lot of the small towns in the Northwest Territories. People buy supplies there and do their trading. They meet old friends they haven't seen for a while and exchange gossip and news. Sooner or later everyone, including the children, winds up at the Hudson's Bay post. If they put your letter up it would be seen and talked about. Chances are you'd eventually get a reply."

"I'll do it!" The boy jumped to his feet.

"No, no, Davey. Finish your dinner first!"

The boy sat down again, laughing. "Okay, but right after dinner —"

The quiet snow that had started on the day of Chen's escape from the trap had marked the real beginning of winter. Through the night the ground turned white and the brush became pillowy humps in the flat land. The flock took wing under the dull sky. Chen, tilting on the rising spiral, could see the pure mantle stretching away into the distance, the edges lost on misty horizons. But the waters of the lakes with their endless ragged shores were black as a starless sky, cold and motionless in the stark land.

The storm increased through the second, the third, the fourth day. The quiet stillness disappeared and the winds became gusty, grew to a gale, sweeping the new snow in clouds across the flats. The fury blew itself out at last and by the end of the week the clouds broke, the air began to clear. The next morning dawned bright and breezy. The sky curved blue and clean, and Mount Shasta was a shining giant on the southwest horizon. Chen strutted and preened and gave his loud exuberant cries under the warm sun. He did not feel the chill breeze through the thick down of his body.

From day to day, from week to week he grew and fattened, until as the end of winter approached he was almost as large and strong as the leaders of the flock.

With determination Mooshnuk fastened her eyes upon the printed page of her book. She tried to match the silent concentration of the rest of the class. If she conquered the eighth grade this year, next fall she would go to live in the town of Inuvik and attend the high school there. The thought filled her with excitement. Her best friend, Nepachee, would certainly be going. For Nepachee school was an easy thing. *Her* mind did not fly on the wind across the wide lands, nor sail the skies with the wild geese.

"Nor," Mooshnuk grimly, silently told herself, "think only of that letter that has been pinned for so many days to the bulletin board at the post."

How glad she had been when first she saw the letter that she had mastered the reading of English. Chen, the beautiful Chen, was safe. She had felt the warmth of friendship in her heart for that stranger who lived so far away. David was his name. A nice name, she had thought, one to fit a boy brave enough to stand before the angry man whose trap he had robbed. Ah, unforgivable sin! Mooshnuk's father lived by trapping and woe unto the one who robbed the traps of the north. She shivered at the thought.

But guilt sat within Mooshnuk's heart also. She remembered the lie to her father. Her cheeks turned red at the thought and her stomach felt cold and sick. Like a picture in her mind she could see again the wounded young gander fluttering to earth, feel again the fear that her father would kill that one named Chen, tell again the lie to Akshuya, her father, who trusted her. Even again see Akshuya looking for that which should fill the cooking pot never guessing that his own daughter had told him a false thing.

She had suffered over the lie even before the letter, but the letter which had made her heart glad at the first reading had now made her face the falsehood. She must answer that one named David, and to buy the stamp she must ask her father for the money and then there would be no way but to tell the whole story for she could no longer stand hiding the lie. With an effort she fastened her eyes on the page of her schoolbook and tried to concentrate as did Nepachee.

At least tonight she would face her father with what she had done and it would all be over! Would he never trust her again?

It was more difficult even than she had imagined. Mooshnuk stood before her father who looked at her with kind eyes, and the words would not come at first. There *must* be some right way to say this thing. But she could find no right way. Finally Mooshnuk looked straight into her father's eyes.

"I did a bad thing, Akshuya," she said slowly, then rushed ahead with the next words. "I told you a lie and so robbed the cooking pot."

There was silence in the room with only the soft sound of the winter wind beneath the eaves of the snug house. Akshuya looked at his daughter for some time. Then he said, "There must have been a good reason, for I have never known you to lie."

"It seemed a good reason to me." Mooshnuk's eyes watered and she wanted to look away.

"When was this untruth said?"

"Not long before we folded the tents last summer. The day you shot the white-cheek and saw me standing on the high ground."

The man frowned trying to remember, then he smiled a little and nodded. "Ah, yes. The day you tried to help us by watching to see where that wounded one hid. But even with your help we did not find him —"

"I did not help. That was the lie. I had watched that one fly for the first time that day, and I had watched many days before as you and my uncles killed that one's father. I know it is necessary that we eat, but I could not bear to see that young one killed. So —" and Mooshnuk shrugged her sturdy shoulders in a kind of despair — "I told you he went one way while in truth he went another. It was like stealing, for I remember that evening it was not only I who went without fresh meat but all the others too."

The long dark arctic night lay silently around the small house. Within, the lights were mellow and the stove spread its warmth. But silence lay here also and grew long as the man sat in thought.

Finally Akshuya arose. He still looked into his daughter's eyes. Gently he laid one hand on her shoulder.

"The letter in the store must be for you. You are the one who named that wild white-cheek Chen."

Mooshnuk nodded but all her words were gone.

Akshuya continued. "You must answer the letter, for the wild one who found a home in your heart has yet another friend in a far place. It is well that you answer this other friend."

"And the lie?"

"Yes, there is the lie." Akshuya stood there for some time, his weathered, leathery face immobile. At last he spoke. "Yes, the lie. As you said, you stole from the cooking pot and there must be repayment. After your lessons each evening you will work an extra time with your mother on the stitching of mukluks to be sold in the store. You will buy something for the family with what you earn and the debt shall be repaid." And now Mooshnuk's father smiled down at her. "Then that one named Chen shall be yours. I shall tell others who hunt that if they see that one with the scar upon his shoulder he is not theirs to kill, for you have worked for him and he is yours."

Mooshnuk threw her arms around her father and now there was no need for words.

8 Yearling Summer

At Tule Lake the short days had become long. By the middle of March the brown earth began to show through the snow, and though the winds were still cold and winter yet held the land there was a feel in the air and beneath the surface of the earth that spring was beginning. The old goose seemed to have no interest in any of the ganders. But those pairs who had been together in previous years became more taken with one another, and often separated from the flock. The ganders would bridle and stretch their big wings and hiss angrily at any male intruder.

Chen, who would not mate until his second year, showed no concern with the excitement unless two ganders claimed one goose and did mighty battle for her. Then, when the flock would gather in an agitated, racketing circle to watch the battle, Chen would add his own loud cries to the general bedlam.

As the days grew longer, warmer, another agitation seized the flock. There was the stirring, the continuous flutterings with uneasy short flights, the gabbling, the cackling, the sharpening of the senses to meet the days of coming danger — the migration excitement!

By the last week in March the skim of ice was gone from the shores of the lakes and it did not re-form during the night. As the front of warm air climbed from the equator up through the subtropics on up, up through the temperate zone, the Canada geese began to take wing. Across the width of the United States the stretching isotherm of thirty-five degrees lifted the flocks and swept them northward. Hundreds of thousands of birds marked the high skies, and in the lands that lay beneath the arrowing flocks came the murmur, the whisper, finally the joyous cry, "Spring! Spring! Ah, the winter is gone once more!"

One clear March morning before the sun had touched even Shasta's crown, Chen's flock took to the skies. Chen, with the others, circled above the land that had held them safe, secure. The vast lakes grew small beneath his gaze, the black highway was a thread with an occasional monster shrunk now to the size of a gnat. The faintest haze of green lay across the fields in those spots that were bare of snow. Only Mount Shasta remained a giant, seeming for a while to spread and grow as the flock flew higher. Even that mighty one finally, slowly diminished as the geese began to beat their steady way northward.

And for this season Chen threw his great cry across the skies with only freedom and joy ringing in it. He was big, and as strong as the older geese, yet he had no cares — no mate to protect, no nesting, no feeding of other than his own large appetite. No safety to guard other than his own. Yes, the yearling geese were the bold, careless, roistering adventurers for this one year.

The flock did not travel so fast as to overtake winter. They were held between the mating and nesting urge and the knowledge that a deadly thrust of winter from the north could destroy them. So steadily they flew but they did not press forward with great speed.

Life was a joy to Chen. The sweeping ocean of air and the wide curve of the world beneath seemed freedom itself. He was tireless, flying day after day near the very head of the V. All seemed easy to him though he was not yet of enough strength or wisdom to take the lead position.

There were resting and eating, and ever the wonderful flying, and for the flock danger seemed not to exist. Even so the miles were long and the constant flying took the winter's fat from their bodies. By the time they had crossed the Canadian Rockies the geese were lean again and the eating now did not return the fat but only gave strength to keep pressing northward. But without the fat, one of those deadly thrusts of retreating winter could kill!

Chen and his brother and sister with the old goose still flew together in the flock, though now it was Chen and not the old one who took the position nearest the head of the V. Somehow the goose seemed weary. Perhaps it was only now that the loss of her mate had left her lonely, for her young no longer needed her protection and care, and this spring there would be no nest to build, no eggs to lay, no new downy goslings.

The spring was deceptively warm and it lured the geese to an ever faster pace. The good weather held even until they had their first sight of the Mackenzie River. Here it wound its broad way through the heavy forest, but the distance was yet long to the coast of the Beaufort Sea and the silty delta lands.

The patience of the flock with the long flight was beginning to wane. Now with restless honking they had pressed forward during the night, finally to alight for food and rest as the sky paled with a calm dawn. Their night's flight had brought them to the edge of the open tundra. When they took wing once more the sun was golden in the southeastern sky. It was scarcely worth note that the sky to the north was dark along the horizon. As yet no winds disturbed the peaceful morning.

When once more the flock settled to earth in the afternoon, the air currents had become capricious, snatching at the birds, breaking the even formation of flight. A few of the leaders began giving their disturbed, restless cries when several times a thin, lashing current of cold reached through the warm gusty air of the storm front. The day of the trap had been the last time that Chen had taken safety as a sure thing. Now he heard the warning cries of the leaders and added his own voice to the racketing sound. But the urge to mate, to nest was with the flock and after resting and eating they were eager to take wing again.

By the time the geese had circled high above the land the gusty currents had joined together and had become a steady thrusting tide of air. With nightfall the winds increased and now the cold was steady and biting. But on the flock flew. It was too late to turn back to warmer climes. Too far north. Too near the nesting grounds on the arctic sea.

The cold deepened. The black gale slashed at them,

hurling its tiny shards of ice at the bewildered birds.
The warmth of spring had been a lie and winter had
returned in all of its fury. It was May, but this was to
be a deadly year. For a time, in the battering winds,
Chen could feel the flock around him. The old goose
flew just behind him and for this moment his brother
and sister were also safe.

Then suddenly the moment of safety was gone.
The steady pounding gale exploded. The winds lashed
wildly, this way, that. Chen was snatched upward
into a black icy void. Thrust sideways. Hurled downward. Snatched aloft again. Once he crashed into another flying thing. One of the flock? Whatever it was
fell away and downward. Chen tumbled about in the
whirlpool of black air and unseen cutting icy needles.
He lost all sense of up and down. He flailed with his
mighty wings. It availed him nothing. Still he tumbled and whirled in the arctic night. Time was endless
as he fought the storm. At last even his terror became
a frozen thing. Only instinct kept his wings moving.
Yet through some miracle he remained aloft. He felt
no pain in his battered frozen body. On he struggled.
The furious elements had stolen his sense of direction.
The storm swept him through the night with awful
speed.

What lay below? The tundra? Was there shelter below in the heathy tundra? Or forest perhaps. There
could be shelter in the forest, or death if impaled on a

jagged branch by the mighty whirlpool of the storm. The arctic sea could lie there in the blackness! Ah, surest death of all! The terrible winds of the north would have pushed the ice southward, breaking great grinding floes from the edge of that eternal jutting wall. What chance would Chen have in the freezing black waters with the murderous crashing blocks pounding in the gale-swept waves!

The storm was an eternity. Chen forced his wings to continue the mighty effort. Ice frosted his feathers, the weight dragged him downward. At last the struggle became impossible, the battle useless. The young gander was forced lower, lower. The wicked currents, the ice were to be the victors. And what lay in the blackness below? Was that muttering, that howling only the storm? Could it be the deadly sea, the cruel ice floes?

Then suddenly in a stunning crash it was over! He had no time to reach with his feet, no time to break the fall. There was the crashing sound, all but swallowed by the voice of the storm, and finally Chen lay still. The solid ground was beneath him. The winds howled overhead, yet here there was a kind of shelter. At least his aching body was no longer pounded by the elements. He could not see what lay around him, but it no longer mattered. The dazed numbness faded to a kind of sleep while the treacherous storm erased the spring and turned the land to winter.

Chen blinked in the pale white light. The winds
had ceased and no sound of the outside world reached
him in this strange place. There was only silence. The
whiteness enclosed him like a small cave and when he
stood up the walls and roof sifted a light dry powder
about him. He was sore and when he tried to stretch
his wings he gabbled a protest at the pain. Each movement brought down more of the dry powdery snow,
and in the odd light he saw that small branches pro-
truded from the walls of the cave and laced the roof
above.

The numbness had left him, hunger consumed him
and his great heart bade him explore this world into
which he had been cast by the storm. But how to release himself from the white domed prison? How
thick was the snow above, and would it bury him forever if he tried to thrust his way through into the
upper air? There were a few pale plants growing on
the floor of the cave. These Chen ate quickly. They
did little to diminish his hunger but they did banish
the weakness.

Now to release himself! He pushed with his beak at
the arched roof. The snow made a choking cloud, then
slowly settled about his feet. The brush above remained a solid mass and though it released the snow
at each touch still the thatch held Chen prisoner.
With impatience he flailed with his wings, but he only
bruised the tips. He honked with frustration and once

again beat with his wings. Now the snow all but buried him, cascading from a side wall in a dry torrent of cold white dust. Desperately Chen tramped up and down in an effort to stay on top of the avalanche. He could not see and could scarcely breathe. When finally the slide ceased and the air cleared again, Chen stood blinking in a shaft of sunlight that streaked down a short tunnel slanting upward to the open air. Perhaps it was the opening Chen himself had made when he crashed through the brush in the dark storm.

After a short struggle the gander stood on the surface of the wintry arctic world. In all directions the land was pure white, blazing beneath the May sun. There was no sign of the flock. Chen threw his loud honking cry across the lonely reaches. No answer came to him. Had all been destroyed by the terrible storm?

He had never been alone in this way before. It was a frightening thing! Still the loneliness would not kill him. But starvation, that was another matter. Food he must have and soon, for the store of fat had been used in the long migration. And the battle with the storm had stolen the last of his strength.

Yet the world seemed only to be made of the merciless snow, and that would not fill his gnawing emptiness. He made several attempts to dig to the heathy growth that must lie below, but to no avail. The drifts piled high made it hopeless. He had no strength

for futile effort, so he thrust the white land from him
and arose into the clear arctic air. The cool sky, inno-
cent of any cloud, arched emptily over the wide fea-
tureless land. He gave one loud hopeful cry but there
was no answer. Had the flock all perished or was it
only that Chen had been swept away to a vacant land!

Yet was it vacant? There below, as he tilted to view
the earth, was a shadowy meandering path across the
whiteness and at the head of the markings was a big
arctic hare. That one had been sadly betrayed by the
warm early spring, for now he had partially lost his
white winter coat and the beginning of the gray
summer one made him plain to see in the snowy landscape. His protection had been the camouflage of his
coloring. Even as Chen watched a fox had climbed
from a burrow in the new snow. In moments it saw
the hare. The chase was quickly over. Now the trail
that was left by the fox was tinged with the blood of
his kill.

Ah, no, the land was not empty. The creatures had
been covered by the storm; but as had Chen, so would
they break from their small separate prisons to become hunted and hunter. There was hope for Chen in
the fact of the hare and the fox. They had survived
and so had Chen himself. Surely there were other
geese, hidden now, but alive. So watching the land below, the young gander sailed solitary in the wide sky.

But even as the fox and the hare had brought hope,

so did they bring a warning, for as always a late storm meant hunger in the land. The fox, the wolf, the wolverine would be searching, searching for enough to fill bellies that would become cruelly empty as the days passed. For the present though Chen was safe. On his wide wings he sailed aloft with sharp eyes watching below for open water or the shadow of growing things thrust through the snow.

Instinct carried him westward. The May sun climbed to its highest point in the southern sky. Already it was working at the snow that yet stretched unbroken below. Chen felt the weakness beginning to spread from his body out along the bones and tendons of his wings. Would there be no end to the snow, must he fly forever! Again and again he sent his lonely cry echoing through the empty world. For answer there was only the silence. On he flew.

He had seen the last of the old goose. She had raised her three young and her gander was gone. There had been weariness within her and only a strong spirit could have survived the awful storm. Yet surely all the flock had not been destroyed!

Chen continued to fly but he ceased giving his loud call. Then finally in the still air he heard the gabbling cries of his own kind. Joyous sound! There against the high blue was a small arrowhead of geese. Weariness gone, Chen thrust himself forward, upward toward the noisy flock. Some had indeed survived! But quickly he found that this was a strange flock. He could have joined them and indeed in his loneliness he did fly with them for a short time. Yet if these had weathered the storm so might his own flock. So again he answered the urge to fly to the west. The sun dropped below the horizon but the white world below reflected the twilight glow for a long time and after that gathered the light of the stars so there was no complete darkness. Several times there were skeins of geese, and each time Chen, despite the weakness, joined them with loud cries of welcome. But always the gabbling birds were strangers.

Again Chen settled to earth. The world grew light long before the sun showed on the southern rim. The storm winds must have swept this spot with brutal force, for here even the snow had not tarried. Eagerly the starving young gander dug in the scant covering. Beneath, he found the bent dried grasses of the old year. Eagerly now he ate and the weakness faded. After resting and eating once more, and yet resting again, his spirits rose and the challenge of his loud cry thrust up his long throat and rolled across the world. As if his cry had been a command the sun blazed its first ray of light into the morning sky.

Instinct suddenly stilled his voice. The almost inaudible squeak of the dry snow reached him. He did not look to see the cause. With no cry he thrust with the new strength of his legs. One beat of his wings.

Two feet above the ground. The angry slashing snap was plain to hear. Another thrust of his wings. Six feet above the ground. He did not look back down until he had finished several more flailing beats. There below, frozen in hungry desperate anger, stood a great arctic wolf, the saliva stringing slowly from her jaws as she watched the gander escape. She watched only for seconds until it was clear to her that the gander was gone and she must look elsewhere for the food to make milk for her pups.

Now there were more birds sailing the skies. The desolation of the storm was quickly forgotten though the cruel starvation that came in its wake would linger through the spring. The terrible winds had plucked Chen from the flock and hurled him eastward. Many birds swept from their home grounds and their own flock would have settled in the new place and joined with the strangers there. But something kept Chen flying westward. By the time the sun had reached its highest point on this day, below and far ahead he saw a long mark reaching from the south to the edge of the flat sea ice. As the sun warmed the surface snow and the slow thaw began, dark spots showed along the depressed white line and stretches of black water appeared.

On motionless wings, Chen turned in a descending spiral, drifting down, down. The urge to fly on was gone. Bent willows humped beneath the snow around

the bases of thousands of mounded islands. The Mackenzie delta country! No need to fly farther. Though
the land was strange with its winter mantle, Chen was
content. Once more with no thought of an answer, he
flung his wild *hauk-hauk* on the quiet air. There was
silence. Then as if in echo to his own voice there was a
faint reply. Again he called. Again the echo. With excitement now he honked again and again. With the
answering calls to guide him he soon saw on a mound
that marked one of the larger islands a small gaggle of
geese, perhaps thirty in all. The birds called eagerly at
that one in the sky and several in their agitation flew
aloft.

Chen glided in and the gabbling geese flooded
around him. They were all young ones of his own
flock. All yearlings. Chen's brother was there but his
sister was gone. Of last year's family first the gander
had died, then finally the goose and that one sister
who had managed to survive all the dangers until this
last deadly storm. Now there were only the two
young ganders left.

The thirty yearlings together were safer than any
single goose alone in the savage land. The birds that
had mated at Tule Lake and had managed to survive
the storm had already chosen, each pair, their own
nesting territory. Only these yearlings remained gre-
garious and free. At least in this year of starvation
they had only their own appetites to feed.

So Chen happily joined those with whom he had flown the long miles. And the yearlings' summer had begun. Now the sun hung longer each day in the sky and the slow thaw of the late false winter had begun.

At first only the deep swift channels of the river were clear of ice. Since only the shallow waters were good for feeding, the yearlings were forced to fly across the tundra, searching, always searching for any sign of green things growing. Sometimes they would find spots where the fierce arctic winds had swept the snow away. Then they would feed ravenously, rooting at the thin white layer to bare the ground beneath. But there was never enough to satisfy the constant hunger and they remained thin. Some grew so weak they were easy prey for starving predators.

Chen survived by his strength and wisdom. Yet even for him there was much danger. One day he and one other of the flock, a young goose who seemed more fearless, less weak than some of the others, became impatient with the meager growth where the rest fed. Gradually Chen and the goose widened their circle of searching and presently found that for which they looked. A jutting of rock and a freak of terrain had formed a shallow open cave and here the snow was merely a thin crust with the late spring growth pushing green shoots into the light. Ah, here was enough for once to fill their crying emptiness!

Now Chen and the young goose ate eagerly side by side, gabbling happily. How good, how good the sweet grass was! They ate until the hunger was only a whisper, ate until it almost seemed the good layer of fat was beginning to form beneath the skin. After the days of starvation it was small wonder they forgot other dangers.

It was Chen who saw the shadow fall across the front of the shallow cave. It was he who turned quickly, feathers bristling, wings outspread to face the danger. His quick whirl stopped the charge of two wolves who skulked just outside. They were so close he could see the red glare of their eyes and the slow saliva in the hungry mouths. Chen's loud angry cry brought the goose to his side. At sight of the brutes so close she added her voice to Chen's racket. With the two angry birds facing them the wolves hesitated.

Only flight would save the young gander and the goose, and even Chen could not fly through the solid stone of the cave roof! But the goose stood staunchly at his side and with the two of·them the wolves were afraid to attack.

The brutes dashed in several times trying to separate them, but to no avail. Neither the goose nor the gander would panic. The only escape was to move from beneath the ledge and rush the wolves. If Chen and the goose were quick and lucky, they could drive those two back for an instant, take wing and escape. There was great danger in doing this. If the wolves lost their fear and refused to give ground they would grab one of the birds at the moment of flight and for that one all would be over. Perhaps the goose would not have the bravery to follow Chen's desperate rush. Then they would be separated and open to the fast circling of the wolves where one would threaten from the front while the other would make the deadly attack from the rear.

But death became more certain with hesitation. So with an urgent loud cry to the goose, Chen rushed forward. There was no need to worry about her bravery! She rushed out into the open beside him, hissing and honking, curving her big wings. Before the fearsome feathered monsters the wolves gave way for that precious moment. Chen and the goose did not pause in the forward rush. Each together pushed mightily with legs, feet. Thrust with flailing wings. In an instant they were aloft together, climbing into the safety of the sky.

The wolves spent little time in mourning the lost quarry but trotted off in their grim silent searching. There would be other game less fearsome, less wary.

After that day Chen and the goose ate frequently together on the far edges of the small flock where food was more plentiful. But they became used to watching for danger together, never eating at the same time, taking turn about at cropping the now burgeoning grasses while the other stood sentry.

Once more during that yearling summer Chen was as near death as he had been when the wolves had skulked before the cave. And his second escape was a miracle for in reality death should have come to him that day.

"I saw that white-cheek that is yours, Mooshnuk," Akshuya said. It was August and the man had been hunting to replenish the cooking pots.

"Chen? You saw Chen today!" Mooshnuk's eyes glowed with pleasure.

"Surely it was he." The man pointed at the two geese he had dumped in the shade of the tent and said, "Before I shot these, I was concealed in the willows beside the great river waiting for some white-cheek to come near for my shot. Finally several of them came sailing across the tundra slanting down to alight on the river that flowed behind me. They would have been yearlings, for all the other geese are still in family flocks with their young not yet quite grown, but these were all large birds. The largest of all flew in the lead position with another close at his wing and the rest sailing some distance behind. 'Ah,' I thought, 'that big one shall be for our cooking pot tonight,' and I swung my gun up for a shot. I could not have missed. But with my finger ready on the trigger and my gaze on that great bird, something stopped my shot. In an instant that wise one tilted away, for he had seen my movement and the other who flew so near him escaped too. It was then I realized the white scar of an old wound was on that lead one's shoulder! That was your Chen. I am sure of it."

"Oh, Akshuya!" Mooshnuk had jumped to her feet and now she threw her arms about her father. "Thank you for not harming him! All summer I have watched for him among the thousands of geese that fly the sky. But I have not seen him and I thought perhaps he was even dead."

Akshuya smiled down at his daughter. His children gave him pleasure. He would miss this one when she was gone from the family in the coming winter. Yet he was proud she had conquered all those schoolbooks in Aklavik and now was ready for the high school in Inuvik. Something, he knew not what, had happened within that funny head of his daughter and finally last year she had decided that school was to be taken with some seriousness.

"Now I can write to David and tell him of Chen!" Mooshnuk's face was glowing with happiness. "He will be glad too that our beautiful gander still sails the sky. Do you suppose, Akshuya, that the boys and girls in Inuvik would like to hear some of David's letters, too?"

"Did you read them to your class in Aklavik last winter?"

"Oh, yes. It was the most exciting of all that was done in class. It was much fun at school then. And I worked harder at my lessons because I wanted to be able to write correctly to David. And now" — she smiled widely, happily at Akshuya, her dark eyes gleaming — "now as if some magic had happened I am ready to go to high school in Inuvik!"

Akshuya laughed aloud, but he looked with affection at his daughter. "You are indeed a funny girl, Mooshnuk. All because of a white-cheek you shall go to high school!"

"And also because of David." And she did not mind Akshuya's laughter because of the warmth and pride in his eyes.

It was the end of August when Mooshnuk made her last trip alone across the heath to the edge of the Mackenzie. Always she said goodbye at the end of each summer to the wide, free country and to the wild ones who lived there. And most particularly to the geese. This year she and her family were leaving the tents early and returning to Aklavik so she would be ready to go with Nepachee and the others to Inuvik. Her heart pounded with excitement at the thought, but even with the excitement, today she felt the sadness that always came at leaving the delta land and the open heathy country.

She had come early in the day while the newly risen sun turned the river channels and inlets to liquid silver and cast long shadows from each hummocky rise across the cool landscape. The summer that had followed the cruel spring had been kind. Even now with the days shorter and each night holding its darkness longer than the one before, the air was soft and the breeze only gently stirred Mooshnuk's shining hair.

Four hours she sat, cross-legged, unmoving, atop the rise where so many months before she had watched the old gander give his life that Chen and the others might live. This year the island had been empty. Perhaps next spring Chen would have a mate. Would he return to the island then? Could that have been a goose that Akshuya had seen flying with the young gander?

She had hoped that she might see Chen just once before her summer was ended. But though she sat all through the day, sat while the long shadows of morning shortened at noon, then lengthened for the setting sun, she did not see the big gander nor the one who flew at his side.

Finally Mooshnuk arose. For a long moment she looked across the delta land.

"You fly there, Chen, with all those thousands of

your kind, even though I have not seen you. Perhaps the one that my father saw still flies at your wing. Anshi, I shall call her, so I may think of you as not lonely in the high skies."

She stood silently for a time before turning and starting back toward the tents. Once more summer had ended and as the seasons changed so did the way of living.

9   Chen's Mate

The weather had continued mild until late September. Not until the first cold blasts of winter did the geese take to the sky. This autumn Chen flew very near the head of the flock, for his wings were mighty and his wisdom great. And just behind him flew the young goose Anshi. Through the yearling summer they had become close, and though they would not mate until their second spring they even now flew as a pair.

As though to atone for the savage spring, nature now let the flock pass along the corridor of its migration with more kindness than usual. Yet even though the weather was mild there was the danger of the hunters. It was on an early morning when this danger again turned to reality that Chen became one of the acknowledged leaders of the flock.

They had flown through the black night with only instinct and the hard diamond stars to guide them, but as the sun reached its first rays to the flock the leader spied a large lake below and ahead. The stretching waters and the reedy shores seemed safe and the kind weather had made danger a distant thing. The grayness of dawn still held the land as the flock wheeled, dropping down, down through the cool air.

They had rested at this spot the preceding fall when the old goose had been alive and Chen had flown safely behind her. Since then he had lived a year of dangers and had learned the hard lesson that safety is never a certainty. The leader of the flock now was a bird of great strength, wise with many seasons behind him. But he had lost his mate in the terrible spring storm and the spark of life burned low within him. Perhaps that is why he did not see the movement in the reeds along the shores as he led his flock sharply down across the morning sky. Chen's quick bright eyes did see the slight strange movement of the reeds where no wind was blowing. In that instant he saw too the blue glint of an upthrust gun barrel. He uttered one wild cry of alarm.

Too late, too late for the old leader. There was the terrible boom. So close! Chen could hear the deadly whistling pellets. With no sound of his great voice the leader tumbled over and over straight downward. There was another shot, and another gander who had flown just before Chen slid out of the flock flailing one good wing while the other, broken, dragged him to the lake, to the rushes where he disappeared.

The flock wavered in panic. With no lead gander they knew not which way to fly. Chen, thrusting with his mighty wings, flew through the wildly milling birds. He sent his great hauking cry again and again into the chill air, even as another hunter stood in the reeds for a clear shot. Brave Anshi had followed close behind Chen and added her voice to his commanding cry. As if by a miracle the aimless fluttering geese were drawn in behind the two purposefully winging ones, drawn in behind as though invisible threads pulled them to follow. Up, up Chen mounted, Anshi matching him wing thrust for wing thrust until they had lifted the trailing V to safety.

After that, Chen, though little more than a yearling, became one of the leaders of the flock and Anshi stayed close on his wing through the days and nights of the long migration. With safety they passed through the golden fields of the Peace River valley and over the lofty crest of the Rocky Mountains. This year the jagged spine was free of storms. They followed the valleys and ridges of the flyway down across British Columbia, they sailed past the glistening slopes of Mount Rainier and Mount Hood and above the gentle green land of the Willamette valley. Finally with weary wings they glided down, down the sunny sky to Tule Lake and Goose Lake and the safe stretching lands and grain fields of the Refuge.

David had returned to the city with his mother and father after the wonderful months with Sam. But there had been the promise of Christmas and the two-week vacation to be spent at the Refuge.

With all trace of his invalid's life gone, David found school and friends and the world in general filled with color and excitement. Yet it seemed forever until December. How good it would be to see Sam again! And Chen, what of the beautiful gander? There would only be those two weeks — what chance would there be to find Chen among the thousands of wintering birds? Perhaps though he would have luck and somehow see Chen and that one Mooshnuk called Anshi.

At last, at last vacation came. Even the train was exciting, for David had never traveled alone. It was late in the day when the toiling engine finally hauled its line of cars up the last of the grade into Dunsmuir.

Snow had been brushing down across the windows

all the way up the gorge, but it had ceased falling by the time David climbed from the train. The platform was windswept and cold, the sun gone for the day. But warmth filled the boy when the station door was thrust open and out strode Sam. The man swept his nephew into a great hug, then held the boy at arm's length to look him up and down.

"Davey, Davey, how good of you to come! How's everyone at home?"

"They're all fine. You'll see for yourself. Mom and Dad are coming up here on the twenty-third and we'll all have Christmas together!"

"Wonderful!"

Sam was still beaming when he took David's arm and hustled him along the platform, around the station building and finally into the green Forest Service truck. "I had business to take care of here in Dunsmuir so I saved it for today so I could pick you up on the same trip."

He started the truck, and by the time they pulled out of the parking area onto the highway that wound its steep way through the mountain town, snow began falling again, clinging in small clots to the windshield.

Sam squinted through the glass at the lowering sky.

"Weather forecast said storm. We may have problems getting back."

"I don't care, Sam. I'm just so glad to be here

again!" But then the boy frowned and said, "Just so long as it doesn't storm for days —"

The man glanced at his nephew and smiled a little. "That gander — you want to see if you can find him again, I suppose."

David's blue eyes were bright at the thought. "I sure do. The girl who put the band on his leg still writes and when I answer her this time it would be pretty nice if I could tell her I saw Chen."

"Mooshnuk? The one in Aklavik?"

"Yes, except she's in a town named Inuvik now, going to high school."

They were silent for a while as the man piloted the truck up and around the grades. The black highway turned gray with a thin frosting of snow and gradually to white as the layer thickened. The air was still and the snow muffled the sound of the winter-tread tires. As the trees and the wide up-sweeping land gathered the white flakes David felt he was in another world of magic beauty.

"Well, you might have the luck to see him." Sam took up the conversation as though there had been no silence and Davey smiled remembering this about his uncle from his long stay at the Refuge.

"There's another one that flies with Chen, Mooshnuk thinks. Maybe a goose. Anyway Mooshnuk calls her Anshi."

Sam shook his head a little. "Geese don't mate until

their second spring. It isn't likely that Chen's paired with a goose so soon."

"You're probably right. Mooshnuk didn't see Chen last summer, but her father did. He said there was another one flying with Chen but even Akshuya only saw Chen once."

The pickup finished the steep climb from the canyon. Here the highway swept close to the base of Mount Shasta but that giant was lost in the hanging clouds; and even in the stretching plateau country beyond, the increasing snowfall obscured the wide horizon. David hugged the quiet joy within himself. The wide, wild, wonderful land! It was more like home than the city had ever been!

Finally, with the miles passing steadily beneath the pickup wheels, he became drowsy, slept, awakened several times at the heavy, laboring roar of the solitary snowplows at their task of keeping the highway open. It was dark long before they reached the Refuge.

The storm lasted for two days, but there was little wind and the snow came quietly down. The lands around Tule and Goose Lakes became a pure unmarked expanse, and finally when the sun rose in a clear sky on the third day David could scarcely endure the glistening brilliance of the landscape when he stepped outdoors.

"Well, at last you can go and look for that gander."
Sam smiled down at the boy as they stood viewing
the pristine world. The man's gray eyes were only
slits, squinted against the painful light, a network
of fine creases marking the weathered skin. "There's a
blind you can use that a photographer built last
year, over near the spot you first saw Chen. Don't be
disappointed though if you don't get a look at your
gander."

"I'll have fun watching even if I don't have any
luck." And Davey grinned cheerfully.

So every day, bundled against the cold, the boy
waited in the blind. After the first few days when the
snow had settled, firmed, he was able to tramp the
roads to other spots within the Refuge where he
thought his luck might improve. The first week passed.
Though the boy saw thousands of the wild creatures
he did not see Chen. Though he eyed the geese swimming the black chill waters and inspected them through
Sam's field glasses when they walked the distant flats
rooting in the snow for the grasses and grain, his gander
did not seem to be among them.

The second week began and Davey knew the time
was growing short. Christmas was at the end of the
week and his mother and father would arrive in only
three days. He looked forward to the fun they would
all have together, yet he did long to see the gander

once more and he regretted the swift passage of the days.

When he awoke on the last day that would be free to search for Chen, he found the sky overcast and a chill wind blowing steadily from the north. He put on the heavy wraps, the mittens, the wool socks and boots, and with the binoculars tucked safely into one of the big pockets of his jacket he headed for the blind. Somehow the watching had become hopeless, and on this day the blind seemed dank, colder than it had before.

"I won't stay long," Davey promised himself, but settled to the scanning of the land through the powerful glasses. Twice on the other side of the lake that stretched before the blind, he saw large flocks of Canadas. If Chen had been with one of those flocks they were too far away to clearly distinguish markings even with the glasses. Finally, though, a third flock took to the water from the far shore and began making its slow way across the lake. Leisurely the geese swam, but their clacking and chattering became audible as they drew nearer.

Davey watched motionless, eyes fastened to the field glasses, searching, searching for the white scar that would mark Chen. Suddenly, to his surprise the churring, gabbling of the geese seemed very near. Impossibly near! Slowly Davey lowered the glasses. With breathless amazement he saw a small gaggle of geese sailing serenely across the water not thirty feet from the blind. All that time he had been so intent on the glasses he had ceased watching the near shore!

Now he sat as unmoving as the blue heron who waited for fish. Only his eyes moved, gazing with intensity at each bird who passed before him. What luck that they swam in a direction that exposed their right sides to him! It was Chen's right wing that carried the scar. The procession of geese continued until perhaps a hundred had passed before the blind. With disappointment Davey watched the last one glide by.

He was on the verge of moving, now resigned to the fact that this vacation he would not see Chen. Yet just as he was ready to give up, something held him quiet for a moment longer. A soft churring had come to him so close that for a moment his heart thudded against his ribs. Seeming scarcely to move, he shifted until he could peer over the raised front of the blind. There, almost near enough to touch, were a dozen geese, obviously of the flock that had just passed in the water.

And the wonder of it! Two walked before the others and the first of these had a white blaze across the right shoulder. About one leg when he raised it high to step carefully in the snow was the dull gleam of metal, and this one was larger than any of the others.

Davey had moved so carefully that the geese did

not take flight. They lingered long enough for Davey to study them in every detail. Yes, that other one did indeed seem to be with Chen. The two stayed close together, churring constantly to each other. He liked to think as did Mooshnuk that Chen traveled the wide skies with a partner beside him. And the spring was really not so far away!

Finally when the geese took to the water and started moving away from the blind, Davey said softly, "Goodbye, Chen. Maybe this is the last time I'll see you. Mooshnuk will be glad to know that you came safely to Tule Lake with Anshi at your side."

Though his voice scarcely broke the silence the geese scolded in alarm, two or three taking wing to skim above the dark water. Only Chen hesitated for a moment as if the sound of the boy's voice brought some memory to him. He gazed back at the shore with bright black eyes. But the one who swam beside him began to gabble nervously and finally he turned and swam off with the others.

10 The Beginning Again

The spring came late that year but with a sudden warmth and a brightness of the sun that turned lakes, ponds, marshy flats to a shimmering glory. The grasses seemed to sprout and become lush, green in a matter of days. And with all the wild things of the Refuge this season of mating was charged with an excitement, an intensity beyond the usual.

There were rustlings and stirrings in the meadows and small piping squeaks and squeals of challenge and battle. The waters of streams and ponds were busy with muskrats and beavers, glossy and bold with the new spring.

And over all the stretching countryside, across the high sky came the dissonant cries of hundreds of thousands of birds. Spring and the ancient miracle again!

Chen and Anshi had stayed together through the winter, but with the mating season a change came over them. Chen grew bold and quarrelsome at the approach of any strange gander. He would stand tall and fearless, the sun striking coppery gleams from his beautiful body. His neck and head were sleek and glistening in the translucent light, the chin and cheek patch clean and white and sharply defined. He would hurl his mighty challenging cry at the intruder, beak wide and fierce, wings arched to their full six-and-a-half-foot span, eyes flashing black fire with his anger.

Few were foolish enough to accept this challenge. There were other geese with less formidable ganders than this one for protector! Other geese, perhaps not so lovely as the softly churring Anshi, perhaps not so strong and rounded nor with daintily stepping, hesitant gait. Yet with all of this charm it was not worth the risk to battle that great gander!

Each day grew warmer; the nights lost their chill.

And as in other springs the migration fever began to sweep across the land. Most of the geese were paired and many had finished their mating before the urge to wing northward drew the flocks into the sky.

One morning with the air cool and sweet, the leaders of one flock sent their racketing cries across the water. In moments the mass of birds thrust the land away, arose with the muffled roar of countless wings, mounted into the rosy dawn, circled up, up, turned toward the north. The gander who led the flock had a white slash of feathers across his right shoulder where the wing met his body.

There was no treachery in the warmth of this spring, no slashing attack of a dying winter to tear the flocks asunder. Chen and Anshi flew at the head of the steadily winging V until they wearied of the effort; then they dropped a little back in line and another leader had the task of breasting the transparent currents. Then another and another, each resting in turn, each ready to share this collective burden of leadership.

And the wide empty sky was filled with the racket of the flock's passing, and earthbound creatures gazed aloft in wonder at the honkers who thus noisily swept springtime with them, erasing the tedious winter.

Because of the lateness of this spring the flocks had not left the wintering grounds until April. This would make their season in the north short, so they pressed forward, flying long hours each day, wearing the winter fat from their bodies. Chen shared their urgency for he and Anshi had had their mating in the sunny meadows beside Tule Lake. Now they must reach the delta land beside the Beaufort Sea to build their nest together and be ready for the laying of the eggs.

It was on a day in the first week of June that the flock wheeled in across the glistening wild land at the mouth of the Mackenzie River. Here too the spring had been late, but now each day the sun shone brightly and its warmth already had cleared the many-fingered delta channels of winter's ice. As the flock circled lower the mated geese began breaking away in solitary pairs.

At a particular moment, instinct pulled Chen away and downward. Anshi stayed close beside him and their wingbeats matched with steady purpose. The big gander slanted across the islands and bars and seaward-rushing waters of the river and at a spot where the delta land touched the heathy tundra he and his mate came to earth. This would be their nesting place! The low sandy island was separated from the continental shore by a swift channel of water, green with the melted snow.

Now with little rest they began gathering the sticks of whitened driftwood and the frame of the nest was set in the center of the island where the reeds and rushes encircled it. They paid no heed to the jaegers, to the kittiwakes, to the mother seals and their pups who lay basking on the sea ice in the cool arctic sun.

Next into the framework of driftwood they thrust the twiggy sticks gathered from the heath, giving no thought to the ptarmigan, nor the snow bunting, nor the silent arctic fox scraggly as spring always found him in the process of losing his fine coat of winter.

Now came the pliable reeds and rushes from the swampy river land, to pad and soften the rough frame of branches and twigs. No time to notice the sandpipers, the godwits, the muskrats busy along the banks.

And last the nest was lined with the down from Anshi's own body. Then they were ready and all that remained was the waiting.

The cool arctic sun hung longer each day in the sky. One morning toward the end of July a young girl made her way across the heath. She moved with grace for beneath the square garments her body was lithe; no longer did she carry the plumpness of childhood. Steadily she walked until she reached a hummocky rise near the edge of the river. She climbed to the top of the rise and shading her eyes with one hand looked at the small island that lay separated from the mainland by a strip of rushing water. As she gazed, unmoving, silent, a shadow swept across the sky. It was a Canada goose and as he sailed lower to light upon the island the girl could see the blaze of white feathers on his right shoulder.

"Ah, you did finally return to the island, Chen!" Mooshnuk's eyes shone with wonder. "And you do fly with beauty as your father did!"

For a long time she stood on the hummock, watching the gander bring the tufted grasses, the crow berries, the succulent water plants to the goose who waited upon the nest.

"You are late with the hatching this year, Anshi," Mooshnuk whispered to the arctic breeze. "May winter be slow in coming for the sake of your young ones!"

She watched until the gander had brought sufficient food, for a time at least, to satisfy the goose's hunger; watched as Chen took up his vigil near the shore of the island. Then slowly, quietly she made her way down the rise to stand on the river bank.

Chen saw her coming. Uneasily he hissed and half spread his big wings. But when she stood unmoving and spoke to him the hiss died in his throat and hesitantly the wings settled into place. His black, wise eyes watched that one who somehow did not seem a stranger.

"I am no longer a child, Chen," she said, "and my time to freely wander the heath is past. Perhaps I shall see you again, but I think not. At least I can tell David that the spirit your father shared with you will now reach further to your own young. For see, Anshi is uneasy upon her nest and perhaps even now the eggs are hatching!"

The girl on the shore and the gander upon the island stood gazing at one another across the stretch of rushing water. Finally the girl turned away and started across the heath. She grew smaller and smaller until the immensity of the land swallowed her.

Anshi moved restlessly upon the nest. Something was happening to that first-laid egg! Presently a scrap of sound was flung upon the arctic breeze. It scarcely creased the silence, but Chen heard it and turned from gazing at the land where the girl had disappeared.